THAT ROCK
DON'T ROLL

THAT ROCK DON'T ROLL

BY DON ALEXANDER

ARCHWAY
PUBLISHING

Archway Publishing books may be ordered through booksellers or by contacting:

Archway Publishing
1663 Liberty Drive
Bloomington, IN 47403
www.archwaypublishing.com
1 (888) 242-5904

Cover painting by Jim Alexander.

ISBN: 978-1-4808-9492-1 (sc)
ISBN: 978-1-4808-9493-8 (hc)
ISBN: 978-1-4808-9494-5 (e)

Library of Congress Control Number: 2020916018

Print information available on the last page.

Archway Publishing rev. date: 1/6/2021

To my children, Debbie, Dan, Dave, and Dixie, and my grandkids, John, Kasie, Jaime, Tim, Ben, and Julie. The best family a man could have, they have always been an inspiration to me. Thank you.

To my Rotary friends, a wonderful organization that saves and improves many lives. Their friendship has been a key to my success in life and certainly an inspiration for being able to continue in the wonderful worlds of sports and life.

To my many friends, especially my extended family, who remained my good friends even after the death of my wife, Gayle.

To Gayle, a wonderful woman who had to put up with all my sports activities and even helped in the TV booth for many years! I had thirty-two wonderful years with her.

To everyone else in my life. I would have to take up this whole book to list everyone that has been so good to me. Thank you all.

ACKNOWLEDGEMENTS

To my writing mentor, TV broadcasting partner, newspaper publisher, and college instructor colleague, Jim Tortolano. I don't know of a better one in those fields, and he is a wonderful person as well.

To my brother, Jim Alexander. A great artist, he painted the cover of this book and contributed many ideas to the cover 's completion.To another great brother, Joe Alexander.

To the athletes—pro, college, and high school—I have interviewed and written about. They supplied the action and stories. I was fortunate enough to broadcast and write about them for twenty-seven years.

To the coaches at the high school level. These coaches make about $1 dollar an hour. (Maybe less) I was most impressed at what they would teach teens about life, let alone about how to lose and win and the intricacies of the sports.

To Sports. Sports teaches everyone a lot more than

what is seen on TV. In high school and college, the athletes must maintain their grades and citizenship. I know for a fact that sports have saved a huge number of boys and girls from traveling down the wrong path. In the pros, they deal with maturity, the public, and sustainability. They can make big money. The vast majority handle it well. Some don't. Therein lies the basis for this book.

BOOK I

1

The football was on the fifty-yard line. A running back for the Orange County Rhinos ran around the left end and broke free for an apparent touchdown. At the ten-yard line, he fell down, listless from head to foot. He hadn't been hit. He was all alone. "What could have happened?" said *Sports Register Magazine* investigative reporter Blake Brennon to his boss, Rex Harrington. Both were watching the game on TV at the sports magazine's office.

"Sounds like something you need to look into," said Rex. "We just got a call from the stadium saying Cadillac Williams has been carried off the field, much to the dismay of millions of football fans watching in person and on TV. The stadium isn't too far. Get down there."

The Orange County sheriff's investigators were still at the new Orange Grove Stadium when Blake arrived. "Tom, what's going on?"

"We're interviewing as many fans as we can, but

there were eighty thousand of them here. It doesn't look like we're going to get anywhere with them," said Tom Stanley, sergeant and an as-needed friend of Blake's.

"I need to get into the locker room, Tom. Can you get me in there?"

"I'll try. It's hot and heavy in there. But the guys know you, and you always help us out. I don't see a problem."

The two proceeded down runway 7, turned right, and then took the elevator down to the locker room. Many news guys and two news women were waiting outside in the hall, but Tom took Blake right in.

"How did he die?" Blake asked no one in particular.

"Hello, Blake," said a voice from behind a training table that had Cadillac Williams on it. "It's me, Lieutenant Blank Smith. How did you get in here?"

"The public has a right to know. I'm in here for the public," said Blake.

"And I look like Brad Pitt," said the rather portly lieutenant with thinning hair and a suit jacket that was begging to be two sizes bigger. "You know the public doesn't have any right to know. That may work with the rookies, but *please*."

"Okay, okay. Just tell me why the guy died, and I'll be a silent fly on the wall."

"You couldn't be a silent anything anywhere! We really don't know. There are no wounds, no holes. I guess it's going to take an autopsy."

Blake looked at the body. It seemed like it was just yesterday that he wrote about the big tailback from Cal-State Fullerton University. He was a college hero and took over as starter for the professional football Rhinos this year, only one year after being the first draft choice of the newest of the National Football League's teams. He was on his way to breaking the Orange County Rhino's rushing record when he went down in this last game of the regular season.

Blake had written about the big, strapping 6'2", 230 pound runningback for three years. Cadillac left CSFU a year early after he was runner-up in the Heisman derby a couple of years ago. He was the first player chosen by the hapless Rhinos, but this year, he beat out Kyle Strogham, and the team made the playoffs. Cadillac appeared a lot in the West Coast edition of *Sports Register Magazine*. Perhaps now he would be on the cover only one more time.

"The Rhinos probably won't go very far now," said Blake.

"They still might win. Strogham is pretty good too," said Blank. "He still holds the team record for rushing. We have a chance!"

Blake replied, "Maybe so, but a lot of us sportswriters and fans will be in mourning. Cadillac was a real role model in addition to a great player."

Blake knew all about the underbelly of professional

sports. He had covered his share of assaults, spousal abuse, drunken driving, orgies, drug abuse, and much more. Blake thought there could be nothing sinister in any of this, but his gut was wrenching a different scenario.

"Blank, I need to file a story today. Give me what you have."

"All I know is that Cadillac broke a long run around left end and was heading to the end zone when he fell down at the ten-yard line. He apparently died instantly, according to the trainer. He tried to revive him. Play was stopped for twenty minutes. He was taken to this room, where he was pronounced dead, but he apparently was dead when he fell."

"Thanks, Blank. Will you call me when you get the autopsy report?"

"I'll try. By the way, I thought you'd have the cheerleaders interviewed by now." Blank smiled.

"That's next. Thanks, Blank."

Blake knew that writing for his weekly sports magazine meant he couldn't scoop daily newspapers, internet, and TV news. But he usually could get more information than the regular news reporters, and sometimes he could get scoops too!

He would always help the local cops if they needed some information that was perhaps not exactly legal for them to obtain. Just last year, a local sports agent/manager was arrested for stealing money from one of his clients. Blake was able to get some incriminating paperwork from the agent's office. Blake said he got a tip and followed his leads.

The judge threatened to put Blake in jail for not revealing his source. Blake cited the California shield law. The judge laughed. Both of them knew that journalists were put in jail all the time, and shield laws mean little. Blake escaped jail that time.

But it was favors like this that made him friends with the local sheriff's office, so it was worth it. Lt. Blank Smith was hardly a friend. They both used each other to get what they wanted.

Blake made his way down to the cheerleaders' locker room. Some of the girls were sobbing, and others looked bewildered. Most were half-dressed at best. Blake noticed Tiffany in the corner.

"I'm sorry about what happened today. Did anyone see anything?" Blake asked. Blake hoped Tiffany would answer. She was a curvy blonde, about twenty-five, with the cutest bared waist on the team. Her breasts were enhanced, but she had such a sweet, feminine way about her. In addition, she actually knew a little about football.

"I just can't believe it! Cadillac was one of the few gentlemen on the team. He ran right past me. He looked great, and then all of a sudden ..." started Tiffany.

"I know, Tiff," Blake sympathized. "That rock don't roll. But is there anything you saw that could help me?"

"Nothing. I didn't hear anything. I didn't see anything, and he died right in front of me. We were doing stunts on that end of the field. We were cheering him on. I just can't believe it."

Tiffany put her head on Blake's shoulder. Blake wished the circumstances were different so he could console her in a more appropriate way. But he regained his senses before he acted on his impulses.

Then Tiffany popped the question. "Blake, can you take me home? I just don't think I can drive."

"Okay, I'll meet you at the employees' parking lot outside of gate 7. You get out of your cheerleader's outfit, and I'll meet you there."

Blake felt guilty about the way he said that, but Tiffany was gorgeous. He couldn't turn her down.

After talking to some of the other girls to no avail, Blake headed up the elevator and out gate 7. To his surprise, there were still a lot of people outside, and the sheriff's department was still busily talking to everyone they could. Blake didn't bother. He would look later at the tape of the game. That should tell him some of what he needed to know.

2

Blake took Tiffany home. He didn't realize she lived in Hollywood, quite a drive from Orange Grove in Orange County.

"Please come in, Blake. I just can't be alone tonight," whimpered Tiffany.

"Okay, but I sleep on the couch," said Blake, his conscience getting the best of him.

"Okay, we'll sleep on the couch. But we'd really be more comfortable in my bed," said Tiffany.

Blake gave in and played out his fantasy with Tiffany. It was the first time he felt augmented breasts, and it really didn't feel that much different from the real thing. Either that or he didn't care. They made love for a long time before falling asleep.

Blake awoke the next morning just after nine, feeling like he had taken advantage of Tiffany and thinking maybe he wasn't the gentleman he hoped he was. But

Tiffany was already up, making him breakfast in a see-through nightie. His conscience again left him to fend for himself.

"Hi, sleepyhead," said Tiffany.

"Hi, yourself. You wore me out last night. I am a little older than you, you know."

"You seemed just the right age last night. How about eggs Benedict?"

"That would be great. I have to tell you—I feel guilty about last night."

"So do I. I took advantage of you, making you stay with me all night. I hope you forgive me."

"Apology accepted," said Blake as he gave up. "Tiff, I really want to talk to you about yesterday. Is there anything you can remember about Cadillac that was out of the ordinary?"

"He felt a little sick before the game. He talked to me as we were waiting to bust through the paper welcome sign."

"You mean like a cold or maybe some aches and pains?"

"No, like sick to his stomach. Maybe he was just nervous."

"Maybe. He was set to break the record yesterday."

Blake's cell phone rang and interrupted their conversation. It was Blank Smith, the sheriff lieutenant. "Hey, Blake, we're going to go over all of the tapes we could find of Cadillac's last run. If you can get here in fifteen minutes, you can view them with us."

"Give me an hour, Blank. To fill in your time, get some footage of other games where Cadillac was on tape, okay?"

"You can get to our office in fifteen minutes from anywhere in Orange County. What gives?"

"I'm in Hollywood, questioning a witness. I'm leaving now. Bye."

"Is that what I am?" asked Tiffany. "A witness?"

"I was protecting your reputation. I never kiss and tell."

"You were protecting your own reputation, and I do kiss and tell. Sorry, Blake."

"That's okay. Just don't say anything negative, okay?"

"There wasn't anything negative. Come again and console me. Here's a Benedict to go."

"Thanks, Tiff. We'll definitely see each other again."

With that, Blake waited for Tiffany to hurriedly get dressed. They got in his BMW and sped down the freeway to the stadium. He dropped off Tiffany to get her car and then sped off to the Orange County sheriff's office in Santa Ana.

3

"Hello, Blake," said Blank. "You look a little disheveled. Rough night?"

"No, a great night. You old married guys forget what it's like. It can be very draining. Anyway, lead on to the tapes!"

Blake saw the tapes of Cadillac running around left end. Cadillac's face looked determined. He looked around, saw he had a beeline to the end zone, and headed for it. Then he stopped, grimaced, and fell down. Motionless. After that, it was CPR and a lot of people trying to revive Cadillac. There was no reason for him to go down.

"Did you get other views during the game?" asked Blake.

"We did. We looked at them already and didn't see anything."

"Mind if I look at them?"

"No, go ahead. I'll be in the other room."

Blake looked at the entire game footage. It showed Cadillac on the sidelines, sitting on the bench with the trainer beside him. The trainer apparently was concerned over Cadillac's discomfort. But Cadillac wasn't rubbing anything. That meant it was internal or pain in the groin. Players had long known that modern TV cameras can see their nose hairs, and they don't pick at those noses or rub *down there.*

But Cadillac hadn't missed a down or looked bad during the game. The trainer looked after other players, and all of them made faces from time to time.

Blake made his way to Blank's office. "What took you so long? Cadillac's run lasted seven seconds," said Blank.

"I watched the whole game," said Blake. "Did you get any personal tapes?"

"No. You would think we would have something with all those cell phones around. But cell phones are far away. We did ask the other TV stations and other news guys to give us anything they have."

"That's good, Blank. But they don't know what to look for. I really don't either, but something has to be there. I do know that rock don't roll!"

"Ever since you got your PI license and took up investigative sports reporting, you've been real uppity. Others of us know a lot too!"

"I know that," said Blake." I just wish the autopsy

11

was done. On TV shows, they could get the results in minutes."

"If we were like TV, we could solve the cases, mostly in an hour. Maybe sometimes in a two-parter. Two hours."

"By the way, how did you get that name, Blank? I've wanted to ask you that for a long time, but the time was never right."

"I was the youngest of ten kids. My mother left the first name blank on the birth certificate. They never could come up with a name. My parents just called me Blank. They thought it was cute. Any other questions?"

"No, that's enough for now. Please call when you hear something."

"I will, maybe," said Blank.

Blake thought he would. After all, he called him about the tapes. But would he call him when the autopsy came in? Blake never counted on anyone except himself. Blake's law! Everyone had a motive. Everyone needed a reason to do something for someone else. It was Blake's job to constantly provide those reasons.

4

B lake decided to make an appearance in his office in Santa Ana. Blake's secretary, Liz, gave Blake a bunch of messages. "Some of these you already got on your texts, but just to make sure ... and Rex wants to see you."

Blake traveled the long corridor to his boss's office, walked past piles of folders, paperwork, and computer discs, and waved hello.

"Hi, Blake. Anything new on the Cadillac case?" asked Rex.

"Not yet. It might be a week or so before anything pops. Then again, it just may be his ticker went out, and that's it."

"Hope not. But just in case, how about looking into Rocket Wallace's kidnapping? I know they found him safe and sound, but rumor has it there was a wrinkle in all of this. No one knows for sure. Go find out what it is."

Blake walked out wondering what the wrinkle could

be. Was Rocket, a local pro football star, set up by his ex-wife? Was insurance involved in a ransom? Was there a ransom? Blake walked into his office. It was a waste of space because Blake only came in when he had to. Blake called Blank.

"Blank, what's going down with our cornerback? I know all about the wrinkle in this case. I just want to get your perspective."

"How did you know?" asked Blank. "Listen, come in and let's talk."

"Okay. And this time, I can be right there. I'm in my office in Santa Ana. It's just a hop and a skip to your office. Bye."

Blake said goodbye to Liz and walked to his car in the garage. The parking pass was long outdated, but the kid in the booth always let him in and out anyway.

Blake pulled up to the sheriff's office and walked into the bottom floor of the three-story building. He was greeted at the front desk by a new receptionist.

"Is Blank Smith in?" asked Blake.

"Yes," said a smart-looking young lady with a tailored suit that tried to hide most of her charms. "He's expecting you. Go right in."

Blake walked into a little office he had been in many times before. But he certainly had never seen the woman in the tailored suit. "Hi, Blank. Who's the woman out front, and what's the secrecy?"

"Her name is Petunia, just transferred in, and how did you find out about the Wallace thing?"

"I have my sources, Blank. How long did you think you could keep it a secret?" Blake had no idea what the secret or wrinkle was, but this technique had worked before.

"You can't publish this," said Blank. "It could hurt people if you did. People might even die!"

"Okay. Tell me what you know and why I shouldn't print it."

Rocket Wallace was the cornerback on the Rhinos. He had disappeared for a couple of days but showed up yesterday.

"As you know, Rocket was found right away. His captors were apprehended, and they didn't get a penny of the one-million-dollar ransom they asked for," said Blank.

Blake thought this was good. He now knew there was a ransom, how much, and the time frame of the kidnapping. "Great. So why can't I print that?"

"I'll give you those details if you don't print how we got to him so fast. That's what I need you to do."

"What's your reason for asking me this?" asked Blake, still trying to figure out what this was all about.

"Because if it got out and kidnappers know about it, it might foil our chances in future abductions. Capisce?"

"Not really. Maybe if the public knew about it, it

would discourage kidnappers. Tell me more so we can come to an understanding."

"GPS found him right away. The kidnappers didn't know what hit 'em."

"But, Blank, GPS is nothing new. Most kidnappers know to get the victims out of their cars quickly."

"You don't really know about this, do you?" asked Blank.

"I do now," Blake said. " I just don't get why you want me to sit on it."

"Gotta go now, Blake. Nice talking with you."

Blake got up and walked out, passing the tailored suit lady. "How about lunch someday?" asked Blake.

"Going to pump me for information like the *LA Times* guy did?" she asked.

Blake liked straight lines but decided to bypass the pumping reference and get her name. "Are you sure Petunia is your real name?"

"You media pigs like that name, don't you?"

"Uh, some other time, Petunia?"

"Listen, maybe I was a little harsh. Actually, my name is Petula. My friends call me Pet. Just remember, if we do go out, no pumping!"

"Agreed. And I like your suit."

"Thanks. And you're not nearly as bad as other reporters that come in here. They all look like they sleep in their clothes."

"Thank you. I think. I work for a weekly sports magazine. Maybe that's why I can change clothes every day."

"Pet!" interrupted Blank. "I need you in here right now." She immediately walked away. Blake thought it was interesting that Blank said her name was Petunia. One day he would find out. But for now, he had other things on his mind.

5

Blake pulled out his cell phone and called his office. "Liz, anything important?"

"Yes, we got a ticket for you for Sunday's game. It'll be at will call under SRM and your name. Take your driver's license and magazine ID. They're getting pretty strict on that. And Lt. Smith called and said you can witness the autopsy tomorrow if you'd like. It'll be at 9:00 a.m."

"Thanks, Liz. I'll be there. By the way, can you find someone who knows about GPS? I need to find out more about that technology. Lt. Smith was real evasive, so something is up."

"Will do. By the way, you have a full-access ticket to the game. Rex thought you might want to snoop around a bit."

"Okay, I'll snoop. But I don't even know if there is anything to snoop about! Bye."

Blake decided to go home—a nice, now-expensive

condo he has owned for years, right on the water on Newport Bay. He couldn't come close to affording it now, but luckily his grandfather had purchased it years ago before the big real estate boom in Orange County. Blake inherited it. With a special California law he could easily afford the taxes.

Blake pushed his access card into the little box by a gate that seemed to take forever to open and let him in. He drove around to the back, parked in his one-car garage, and traveled the back stairs up to his three-story condo.

Blake liked his place. He has nine televisions, including one in each of his three bathrooms. He has four radios, plus an entertainment center with a great sound system that played in all of the rooms. Blake watched only one TV when a date might drop over. Otherwise, it was many TVs on all at once. After all, sports is his business. He had to watch sports.

Blake walked up the bottom stairs to the middle section of his condo that held most of the televisions and his kitchen and living room. Once in, Blake slumped on the couch and thought about his prospective stories. One dead ballplayer, one kidnapped player, a playoff game coming up, and a woman in a tailored suit he couldn't get out of his mind.

Blake decided that the game could provide a good story, and he could get some antidotes on Cadillac from some players. But he didn't think long before the phone rang.

"Hello, Blake?"

Blake answered affirmatively.

"This is Pet. I just feel awful about the way I treated you. I'll go out to lunch with you. How about tomorrow?"

Blake was a little puzzled about this turn of events, but he thought himself to be a charmer, and most women did respond. Better than Pet. And Blake was a reasonably good-looking man in his midforties. Blake said he would meet her at the Bat Rack at noon the next day. He should be done with the autopsy by then.

Blake awoke on Saturday. He showered and put on his best weekend digs. He didn't need to impress the medical examiner, but later, he was going to see Pet. He walked confidently to his BMW, wishing it were a Porsche so he could really impress Pet. Out of the security gate, he went to the coroner's office in Santa Ana. He rang a bell inside and was greeted by Dr. Gordon Fukumoto. "You must be Brennon. Come on in. A cop is in here already."

A sheriff deputy was there too.

Blake was stunned by the sterile-looking metal walls and tile floors. He was blinded by the lights. The autopsy rooms on the TV cop shows were dim and spooky. Not there. On the table was Cadillac Williams. To Blake, Cadillac looked at peace. He didn't have that competitive look on his face—just a serene look that made Blake feel calm himself, until Dr. Fukumoto briskly raised the sheet from the body and started cutting.

"You going to be okay, Brennon?"

"I think so. I'll just stay back here out of your way. By the way, why is it so bright in here?"

"We don't want to miss anything. Need plenty of light. We've got to find out why this guy died." Dr. Fukumoto looked over the body, noting tattoos, scars, and hair and checked the toe tag to make sure this was the right corpse. He took pictures all along the way.

Dr. Fukumoto then cut the familiar Y on Cadillac's chest. Not too deep. He didn't want to cut the organs yet. There was no bleeding, or very little of it. Blake knew when the heart stopped pumping, the blood stopped flowing.

"I've already read the decedent's medical records and have opened the chest cavity," said the doctor into a microphone attached to his jacket like the police and firefighters used. His words were recorded for future use. Dr. Fukumoto turned off the microphone by pressing a lever with his foot. "Brennon, if you or the officer have questions, raise your hand. I'll might even ask you questions. Otherwise, I will be mumbling into this mic."

So far, Blake was handling it pretty well. This was his first autopsy, and the smell wasn't as bad as everyone had warned. Blake looked intently as the doctor took out the heart and lungs. Blake didn't realize they looked connected. Blake listened.

"I'm sectioning the heart and lungs, looking for pulmonary disease, edema, signs of suffocation, drowning and pneumonia, arterial sclerosis, blood clots, and valve damage."

Blake saw him sectioning the organs about a half inch apart but not all the way through. Blake raised his hand and his eyebrows.

"This way, we don't have a lot of pieces. It can remain intact, easier to put back into the cavity," said Dr. Fukumoto, without even hearing the question. Back on the record, the doctor said there was nothing significant about the heart and lungs.

"Now I have the heart in my hands. Say, Brennon, you have gloves and gown on. Come over here. You want to hold a heart?"

Blake might have done it, but the cop said he couldn't because of the chain of evidence rule the officer was there to protect. But Blake did take a closer look before the medical examiner put it back in the body.

Dr. Fukumoto then carved up the liver, which was just as slimy but bigger than Blake imagined. Then it was on to the kidneys, spleen, and other things Blake didn't even know existed.

"Well, let's see what's inside the stomach," said the doctor. "I don't expect any food because most athletes don't eat before a game. But there is some liquid in here that looks funny." He put all of the stomach contents into a jar and set it aside.

"Now let's see what's inside his head." The doctor was careful to cut from the back of his head along the hairline and then pulled the skin flap forward, as if Cadillac wore a mask. This made Blake a little queasy. The doctor looked like he enjoyed Blake's discomfort.

"The reason we do it this way is we can pull the flap back when we're done and preserve his face for a funeral. I will now look at his brain." The doctor used a saw to cut into the skull of the former great running back. Interestingly, the blade automatically stopped when it touched the brain. Blake raised his hand and was answered before he could ask the question again.

"This saw is used in brain surgery on live people as well. It will not cut anything but skull. Pretty slick, huh?"

The brain was lifted from its home and carefully sectioned about a half inch apart, again not cutting all the way through. The doctor was looking for aneurisms and other brain trauma. "The only trauma I can find is old scarring from concussions. I don't see any of that on his medical records, but he sure had a few. Otherwise, everything looks good."

Dr. Fukumoto carefully reassembled the brain and put it back in the head. Then he glued the skull back and pulled the flap of skin back over the head after checking for eye socket and nose damage. There was none, except for what he caused. It didn't take long to sew the flap back.

The doctor then carefully put the organs back in the chest cavity, roughly where they belonged. "I don't have to put them back in the right places, but the cavity is there, and they fit perfectly."

Blake watched as the doctor loosely stapled the chest shut and pulled the sheet back up over the body.

"Brennon, I don't see any problems, but the toxicology report might show something in his blood or stomach contents. I'll send it right out."

"Thank you, Doctor. I can't wait to see that. I appreciate you letting me look in. It was my first."

"You did pretty well. A lot of times, we have to drag the semiconscious first timers out of here. You did well!"

Blake waved as he threw the gown and mask into the receptacle and walked out to his car, with just enough time to get to the Bat Rack to see Pet. He wasn't sure how the food would look after what he just went through.

6

Pet was already there dressed in tight pants and a T-shirt that didn't go all the way down to her waist. Her long, blond hair was down, and she looked even more beautiful than when he first met her. Blake thought to himself he must really be the ladies' man. She couldn't wait to see him.

They sat down at Blake's favorite table, right in front of four TV sets.

"Hi, Blake. This is a nice place. Good choice! I want a tuna sandwich, hold the mayo, and diet cream soda."

"Uh, hi to you too and okay." Blake ordered a pastrami for himself.

Blake waited for the food, which came out pretty fast. He sat down and started a pastrami sandwich that was much too big for his mouth.

"Pet, the first thing I want to know is your name. I know it's not Petunia."

"Close. It's Petula. You know, like Petula Clark, that old singer? Blank just calls me Petunia because it's easier to remember."

"Great. It's nice to see you. What made you decide to call me last night after the cold shoulder you gave me at the sheriff's office?"

"Blank told me to call you to find out what you know about the Rocket kidnapping."

"Boy, you sure are straightforward. I thought it was because of my boyish charm and good looks!"

"Hey, I could have just called you. I didn't have to meet you on my day off, you know."

"Okay. I guess we've had enough small talk. I know everything about it. Tell me what you know so I can get it right in my story," said Blake.

"Before we start, you know how you bloats go to school and learn how to ask tricky questions?" asked Pet.

"Don't know what you mean," Blake answered, having heard another hint of her British ancestry.

Pet said, "Yeah, well, bobbies go to school and learn the same tricks for two reasons. One is that we interrogate bad guys, and two, we learn how to answer attorneys and reporters."

"But I'm innocent!"

"Your eyebrows are so high when you say that I think they're going to fly off your face!"

"Okay," Blake conceded. "Here's what I know. You

found him with the GPS. I just don't know what is so secretive about that. It's common knowledge, even among kidnappers, that a lot of cars have a GPS. They even put them in briefcases and cell phones. So what's the secret?"

"You are so full of blarney, Blake. Let's forget about GPS and use some of that on me!"

"If I do, will you tell me the secret?"

"Not on your life. But we can have fun anyway."

"Okay, next week, we'll have fun. By the way, you're not a cop, are you? I thought you were a receptionist."

"Looks that way, doesn't it? I would really surprise a bad guy coming in thinking I was just a defenseless receptionist, right?"

"You are a tough nut to crack, Pet. But I'll take another shot. I'll call you next week. We'll see if a little wine will pry some answers out of you!"

"Are you sure it's answers you want out of me, Blake?"

"I'll take the fifth on that. See you next week."

Blake walked slowly to his BMW, while Pet drove away in her Porsche. Blake needed a lot of answers about two football players, and he was intrigued with Pet. He was really sorry the autopsy didn't show more. He hoped it would all come together next week. Blake went home.

7

To a sports reporter, Sunday is like normal people's Friday. Blake still hated to get up on Sundays, especially alone. But today was the second round of the playoffs. The Rhinos were favored, slightly, and were playing at home.

Blake dressed in his neutral brown pants and tan alligator shirt. He didn't want to appear partial to any team, but he had followed the Rhinos for a few years and hoped they would win. It would be a lot easier with Cadillac in there, but Kyle Strogham had played well in the first round last week.

Blake threw a couple of waffles in the toaster and plugged in the coffee pot. A few minutes later, he was on his way to Orange Grove Stadium. He parked and went to will call to pick up his pass. He then walked through the media entrance.

It was two hours before game time, so Blake decided

to visit the Rhinos' locker room, where he literally bumped into Bubba Alexander. Bubba weighed in at 305 pounds and anchored the offensive line for the Rhinos.

"Sorry, man," said Bubba. "I'm getting my game face ready for this one. I don't see nobody!"

"No problem, Bubba," said Blake. "How's the team look?"

"We're ready, sir," said Bubba, apparently surprised a reporter would continue talking to him. After all, he was only a lineman.

"Everybody's healthy, except Cadillac of course. Man, whatever happened to him?"

"Not sure, Bubba. I hope to find out the results of the toxicology report this week. Do you know any reason why he might have toppled over like that?"

"No way, except he had the flu all week. Maybe it caught up to him."

"I doubt that would do it, but thanks, Bubba. By the way, who's that guy over there talking to Strogham?"

"Oh, that's Doc, our trainer. Good man. Gets us whatever we need."

"I don't wannna know," said Blake.

Blake walked over to a balding, thin, energetic man in very good shape for being about sixty. He was stretching Kyle Strogham's leg muscles, a common practice to lessen the chance of cramps and muscle pulls during the game.

"Hi. I'm Blake with *Sports Register Magazine*. I'd like to talk to Kyle."

"Not right now," said Doc. "I'll be through with him in a few minutes. This guy is the star he was last year, so you should interview him."

"What is your name, Doc?"

"Same as his, Kyle Strogham."

"You're his father?"

"Sure, everyone knows that. Where you been?"

"I've seen you around, but we don't usually interview trainers. Any idea what happened to Cadillac?"

"Can't figure it. He seemed in great health all week. I guess he had a bad ticker."

"You guess? Aren't you the doctor?"

"I'm no doctor. I'm a trainer. The guys call me Doc because I fix 'em up when they get injured. But if it's broken bones or other stuff, I send 'em to the doctor. Their physical exams are done by MDs, not me."

"Did you give anything to Cadillac for the flu?"

"What flu? Cad was fine."

"Someone saw you give him an injection before the game," Blake lied.

"Who told you that? Wait, I remember. I gave him a B_{12} shot. It helps these guys. It's all cool with the doctor."

"I'm sure it is, Doc. I'm sure it is." He looked at Doc's son. "Hey, Kyle, or should I say Jr. Are you ready?"

"Ask away," Doc answered for him. "Ask away!"

"This is a big break for you, isn't it?"

"No one likes to play because someone else is injured. But I'm a good back. I proved it for several years," said the running back.

Doc broke in. "Hey, we're going to play a big game. I don't like your tone. What are you getting at, whatever your name is?"

"My name is Blake Brennon, and I find it interesting that Kyle is playing because Cadillac was injured—I mean dead."

"Hey, these guys are programmed to say that. Of course, the good ones want to play. And yes, they have a good chance of doing that with all the injuries in the league. This was, of course, tragic," said Doc.

"Thanks for the interview, Kyle. Maybe I can even talk to you after the game."

Blake thought it was strange that Doc interceded like that, but Blake had never had a child, so maybe that was normal. It was time to go to the press box, which meant a three-tier elevator ride up to the club level.

Blake got out and paid five dollars for his spread of greasy stuff in the media lounge. Actually, it was just a room with picnic tables and chairs with a buffet fit for a sportswriter.

Professional sports teams had to charge the media people, so it didn't look like they were taking gifts from the owners. Blake thought that was funny because a couple of hot dogs and a Coke wouldn't change much about who and what he or other reporters wrote about.

A couple of writers a few years back had been treated to much more in the way of feminine company, and that put them in awkward circumstances when the owners asked them to put a lid on some things. But Blake hadn't heard of much of that going on anymore.

The Giants decimated the Rhinos, 33–14. Strogham Jr. didn't look great, and that ended the Rhinos' season. Blake interviewed a few players and filed his story about how Cadillac Williams would have benefited the team both in performance and leadership. Blake hoped he could write a lot more about him soon.

8

The next morning, Blake was awakened by his cell phone rather than his home phone. It was his secretary, Liz.

"Hi, Blake. I've arranged a meeting with a GPS guy up in San Jose, just outside of San Francisco. Your flight leaves at noon."

"Hey, this is my Saturday, even if it's Monday. Just because you guys don't work weekends!"

"Boss wants some good stories from you. All he's been getting lately is what any newspaper writer could get. Capisce?"

"What's with this word, *capisce*? Anyway, fax me over the eticket info and where I'm supposed to go. Thanks, Liz."

Blake got up and noticed he had a message on his home phone from yesterday. He rarely got a call there, except from the magazine, as he always gave out his cell phone number. Blake pushed the *play* button.

"Good evening, Blake. This is Pet. Thought you might want some company tonight. Guess not. What a pity."

Blake liked everything about Pet—her voice, her beauty, everything. But how did she get his home phone number?

Blake dialed her home. Pet answered. "Why, hello, Blake. Where were you last night?"

"I'm a sports reporter. I was covering the big game. How did you get this number?"

"Oh, I must have used my connections at the sheriff's office. You didn't answer your cell."

"No, I had it on vibrate. Was that you buzzing me all night?"

"I was in the mood to buzz you all night. Your loss. Next time, answer your vibrate. Anyway, how about tonight?"

"I'm going up north. Can I get a rain check?"

"Where are you going?"

"San Jose. On business. I'll call you tomorrow."

"I'll give you my home number."

"I have it. Besides, when you call me, your number is on my phone."

"Want to bet?" asked Pet.

Blake got her home number.

Blake got dressed and made the short trip to John

Wayne / Orange County Airport. The facility was not nearly as big as Los Angeles International and was easier to get in and out of. Blake got out his ticket and then waited a long time to get through the security line.

Blake boarded the plane and got into seat 11A. It was economy coach, but the trip was only a little more than an hour away. In San Jose, Blake got a taxi and made it to Beacon Industries. The only thing Blake knew about GPS was that auto manufacture's cars used it to find addresses. He needed to know more.

Blake walked in. "I'm here to see Dr. Roger Garmin."

"Yes," said the brunette behind the computer. "Go back to the third office on your right."

Blake entered the office of Roger Garmin. He looked immaculate in a Versace suit. He was about forty years old. Blake expected something else.

"Come in, Mr. Brennon. Your secretary said you wanted to know all about GPS. May I ask why?"

"I'm a writer for a national magazine, and I just need to know the latest about this."

"Yes, I know who you are, Mr. Brennon. But you are a sportswriter. Why GPS?"

"It's just fascinating. What is it?"

"You are hiding something, Mr. Brennon, but I will play along. There is nothing I will tell you that is not public knowledge. Global Positioning System is a satellite method that uses satellites that circle the globe twice a day in a very precise orbit and transmit signal information to earth."

"So the satellite is programmed to zero in on something?"

"Actually, it takes three satellites to do a 2-D position and four to determine a 3-D position. It can be done in seconds and is very accurate to within fifteen meters on average. Am I losing you, Mr. Brennon?"

"No, Dr. Garmin. Or maybe yes. I kind of figured all of that. Is there anything else I should know?"

"Here is some information I had typed for you. Sorry I couldn't be more helpful."

"That's okay. I really wasn't sure what I was looking for. By the way, what are those dot-like things you have on your desk?"

"Those are just the latest receivers. We're trying to make them smaller every day."

"You mean you could put that little receiver on a car, and the satellite would be able to pick up its location?"

"You don't need this for use on a car. We have receivers as big as a matchbook for that. Ones smaller than this one can be used in the body. In a tooth or elsewhere. Kidnapping has become a problem in the world. This will stop it cold!"

"Are you telling me you could put this in your tooth, put a cap on it, and you could be picked up by satellite?"

"You got it, Mr. Brennon. We've come a long way from the toaster-size transmitters, haven't we?"

"That's for sure, Dr. Garmin. That's for sure. Thank you for your time. I didn't know what I came for, but now I know I got it."

Blake left Dr. Garmin's office with what he thought was a key to a big story. This would be a blockbuster if he could prove that the Orange County kidnapping of Rocket Wallace was solved using this new technology.

Blake was smiling all the way home, but he knew he had to dig a lot more to prove his theory. This would be a great story!

9

Blake awoke the next morning with his cell phone showing two messages—one from Blank's deputy, Pet, and the other from Tiffany. Blake called Pet first.

"Hi, Pet. What's up?"

"I thought we could meet for dinner," she said. "How about at the Riviera tonight?"

"Sounds great. Want me to pick you up?"

"No bloody way. Not yet. Let's take our cars separately and meet there, okay?"

"Sure. See you there at seven?"

"Great, see you there."

Blake had wanted to meet with Pet anyway so he could pump her about the GPS story, as well as the Cadillac Williams situation. And she really intrigued Blake with her sassiness and great looks. So he put on his best duds and found himself in the waiting room at the Riviera, a classy French restaurant.

Pet was twenty minutes late but came in and dazzled Blake in her simple red dress that was very low-cut and showed she had no flaws anywhere.

Blake and Pet were seated next to the fireplace, and the ambiance couldn't have been better for a romantic evening. Blake thought he might save his questions for another time, but Pet started it as soon as the wine had been poured.

"Blank wants to know what you are going to do with the GPS story involving Rocket Wallace."

"No small talk first?" asked Blake.

"Let's get this business out of the way first. Then we'll see about your small talk," answered Pet in a way that seemed to joke about his manhood.

"I'm going to write the story. I know Rocket had a GPS transmitter on his body, and I'm going to write it that way."

"But Blank told you it would put other athletes in danger, as well as politicians and other people."

"I think the opposite," Blake said, trying to keep his eyes above her neck. "I think it will be a deterrent. Can you please give me the location of the GPS on his body?"

"I can't do that. If it ever came out I gave it to you, I would lose more than my job. I won't elaborate."

"If you did tell me, I wouldn't tell a soul. You know judges have tried to make me talk, and I never have."

"I can't tell you, Blake. But if you get it on your own, it would really put some *teeth* into your story."

"Thanks, Pet. I won't bug you anymore. I don't want to put you in jeopardy. Now let's talk about us and what we want to order."

"Sounds great, Blake. I can't wait to sink my *teeth* into the Chicken piccata."

"I get it, Pet. Thanks. Have whatever you want. It's on me."

Blake was dying to get Pet out of that dress, but tonight would not be the night. After a great dinner and admiring her slightly British accent for a couple of hours, Pet said she had to go home—alone.

"Let's do this again," Pet said.

"I'd love to. Anytime. Even now."

"No, I'm full now. I'll call you."

"Okay, Pet. By the way, any news on the autopsy?"

"I think it came in. Call Blank tomorrow."

Blake walked Pet to her car, and they had a long kiss goodbye. It wasn't long enough for Blake, and in the back of his head, he was never sure if she was working or just dating Blake. Of course, he was getting information out of her too. Time would tell. Meanwhile, he was sure that the GPS was implanted in Rocket's tooth, but Blake would have to collaborate Pet's hints so as not to implicate her at all.

10

The next morning, Blake placed a call to Beacon Industries to see if they sold a GPS to the Rhinos' cornerback. They immediately transferred the call to Dr. Garmin. Blake knew Dr. Garmin wouldn't give him anything unless he played him a little.

"Dr. Garmin, nice to talk to you again," said Blake.

"Nice to hear from you, Mr. Brennon. How can I help you?"

"Rocket Wallace raved about the little transmitter you put in his tooth. He wanted me to tell you what a great job you did."

"Thank you, Mr. Brennon. I'm surprised he said anything. The Rhinos told me they wanted to keep it quiet."

"It got out, so the team wanted to get the proper facts out to a respected magazine like ours. You know how some of those tabloids fabricate stuff."

"Yes, I do. Actually, I heard the dentist put it in his

molar. I just designed it. Or I should really say *we* designed it here at Beacon."

"Of course. I didn't mean to imply you practice dentistry. Now, who was that dentist?"

"Mr. Brennon. You should work on that memory of yours. The team dentist, Dr. Kunihiro, would really be mad if you forgot him in your article."

"You're right. He would be. Can I use your picture?"

"As long as it's out, I can't see any harm in getting us a little publicity. Your magazine is nationwide, isn't it?"

"You bet," said Blake. "Including Alaska and Hawaii!"

"I have a picture I can email you. Can I send a bio of me and the company?"

"You bet," answered Blake, even though he had both. He didn't want to alter a rock that was really rolling!

Blake gave Dr. Garman his company email address and thanked the good doctor for the information. Blake now had his story confirmed. He could now write a collaborated story. But he wanted more.

11

Blake had the private telephone numbers of all the players. He called Rocket but had to leave a message. He called Dr. Kunihiro and did the same thing. It was finally time to call Tiffany, his favorite cheerleader.

"Hi, Tiff. Sorry for the delay in getting back to you, but I've been busier than a one-armed wallpaper hanger."

"That's okay," she said. "How about a little action tonight. I'll even come to your place!"

"I'm right in the middle of—"

"Blake, I've got some information about Cadillac. If you're as good as you were last time, I might help you!"

"Sounds good to me. How about meeting you at the stadium. Press entrance?"

"See you there at seven!"

"Okay, bye."

Blake knew he would never have a real relationship with Tiffany, but she had to be the cutest cheerleader in history. And who knew? She might even have some information for him.

Blake was jogged out of his fantasy with a ring on his cell phone. Liz told him Lt. Blank Smith wanted to see him.

Blake raced over to the sheriff's office and immediately saw Pet. Pet started the conversation. "I might let you take me to dinner tonight. Are you busy?"

"Actually, I have to work tonight. How about tomorrow or the next day?"

"I'm busy those nights. We'll see about the bloody future."

"I'm so sorry, Pet. I just can't get out of this interview tonight. Please forgive me. I'd love to see you." Blake wished he hadn't made the date with Tiffany.

"Must be some long interview. I hope she's pretty!"

"I assure you I have to get the last piece of my story and—"

"I do hope you get your last piece, my dear!"

"Uh, thank you, Pet. I'm here to see Blank."

"Go right in. He's expecting you." Pet's voice got colder than Blake had ever experienced. Even when he first met her. Blake walked past Pet's desk and knocked on Blank's door.

12

"Come on in, Blake. How about some coffee?" said Blank.

"Great. Black please. What do ya know?"

"I've got the autopsy on the Williams case."

"Wow, I thought it would never come. How was he killed?"

"Potassium. A lot of it. Apparently, according to the ME, it works faster during exertion. When Williams made that long run, it was just too much for the heart. It started beating faster than it could handle."

"But can that happen with just one pill, or whatever?" asked Blake.

"No, it would have to be given over at least a week's time. Be given in stronger and stronger doses. Know who wanted to kill this rising star?"

"To be honest, the only guy I can think of that would benefit from his death is Kyle Strogham. Kyle was replaced by Cadillac Williams as the starter just as Kyle was positioning himself for the big bucks after this last year. But would he kill for that?"

"I dunno, Blake. Can you nose around a little before we barrel in there? I trust you can hold this from your magazine until we are a little further ahead."

"I will, Blank, but you have to promise not to leak this to anyone. It would compromise my investigation as well."

"I told everyone to keep the lid on. But you know how it is. We all don't have much time."

"Give me a few days. I'll nose around to see what I can find before evidence disappears waiting for search warrants."

"Great, Blake. But remember, you give all information to me. Don't hold back."

"I gotcha, Chief." Blake was crossing his fingers, and he knew Blank wasn't a chief. But all was fair in murder and news reporting.

"By the way, Blank, I have to talk to you about something. I hope you won't be upset," said Blake.

"Now, what could you do to possibly upset me, Blake?"

"Well, the Rocket Wallace story will be out soon. I know all about the GPS in the tooth and your department's great work on getting him back. I just believe that the story will act as a deterrent, and besides, everyone is talking about it. I have to print it."

"Well, well. Did you get anything from this department?"

"No, I did not."

"And the story will indicate we did not help you in any way?"

"Yes, it will."

"Then you have to do what you have to do. If we did help you, I wouldn't want that out. But if we did help you, you owe me one, right?"

"Yes, that would be the case if you helped me, but of course you didn't. I don't suppose you have anything to add to my story aside from the facts, including the manufacturer and the dentist."

"I'll give you a copy of the police report just so you can get everyone's name right and play up our officer's courageous rescue where nobody got hurt and the bad guys are in jail."

"Sounds great. But why the change of heart? Why are you helping me?"

"I'm not helping you, and the story would probably leak soon anyhow. I'd rather it be written by you than some of the other schlocks in your business."

"Uh, thank you. I think. I'll start working on the Cadillac case right away and report back to you."

The two shook hands, and Blake left the office, having to pass Pet on the way out. "Thanks for everything, Pet. Please don't be mad at me. I want to go out with you more than anything. Blank just gave me work to do for him."

"That's funny," said Pet. "You had your appointment before you went in there. No problem. I'm sure I can find company tonight. Bye."

Blake left the sheriff's office with his head feeling like a watermelon in a Gallagher's act. Gallagher was a comedian who smashed watermelons on stage. Why the change of heart by Blank? Did Pet intentionally give him the teeth information, or was it at Blank's orders? Blake was used to playing people, but was he now being played? Somehow that rock don't roll.

Blake called Dr. Kunihiro and got the information he needed. Kyle Strogham Jr. was apparently out of town, and none of the other team members wanted to talk. Blake had enough for a great story. He would start it today and complete it tomorrow, just in time for this week's magazine.

Blake called Liz to inform Rex that he might want to hold the cover. It would be an exciting story and give him time to work on Cadillac's story. Blake had a date with Tiffany, the sexy cheerleader, and life was good.

13

Blake entered the Orange Grove Stadium parking lot at 7:00 p.m. It was empty and a little eerie since he hadn't been to the stadium at night when there was no game going on. He drove to the front of the stadium and saw a new SUV parked right outside gate 7. That had to be Tiffany.

Blake parked alongside her vehicle and wondered how she could afford such a car, but he put that aside, as he was looking forward to their date. Blake got out of his BMW and approached her car.

"Hey, Tiff! Open the door. Your lover is here!" Tiff didn't open the door, so Blake opened it and couldn't believe what he saw.

"Tiff, Tiff, are you okay? Tiff?" But Blake saw the bullet hole in her head and her lifeless body sitting in the driver's seat. Tiffany was dead.

Blake immediately called 911 and asked that they

send out Lt. Smith, if possible. Blake pocketed his cell phone and looked around at the crime scene. Tiffany's purse was sitting on the passenger's seat.

Blake put on his gloves and opened the passenger door and looked in the purse. Right on top was a piece of paper with some words scribbled on it: "Tortolano, steroids, points." Blake put the paper back in her purse, placing it exactly where it had been. He closed the door, ditched the gloves, and wrote the words in his notebook.

By then, a sheriff's car came up. An officer asked Blake to get away from the car. He did that, and soon a yellow tape surrounded Tiffany's car and Blake's. Blake stood outside the tape, and a few minutes later, Lt. Blank Smith arrived.

"What did you do?" asked Blank.

"I had a meeting here with Tiffany, and this is what I came upon! I can't believe she's dead!"

"Did you call 911?"

"Yes, I did."

"I figured that. I don't get called at home on many 911 calls that ask for me personally to respond. What do you think this is all about?"

"I don't know," answered Blake. "I really can't figure this out. Who wants to kill a cheerleader? It makes no sense!"

As Blake was answering questions, another officer in a business suit showed Blake and Blank the paper with the words on it. "Does this mean anything to you? After all, she was coming to see you. And why was she meeting you?" asked Blank.

"Let's see those words. *Tortolano, steroids, points.* I have no idea. We were meeting to go to, ah, my place."

"You don't mind taking me to your place instead, do you, Blake?"

"It's not exactly what I had in mind for tonight, but sure. Let's go."

Blank whispered some instructions to two other cops and then jumped into Blake's BMW, and the two of them drove to Newport Beach.

Blake pulled up to the gate and could see the look on Blank's face. "My grandfather bought this condo in the seventies when it was really cheap. The Prop 13 taxes are really cheap and—"

"You don't owe me an explanation. Just show me this love nest of yours," barked Blank.

Blake parked the car, and he and Blank entered Blake's condo. It was very nice inside, with the lights turned low and wine chilling in the sterling-silver ice bucket. Music was softly playing as they entered Blake's home.

"Wow, no wonder you get laid so much, Blake. How about some wine?"

"Well, uh, okay, Blank. What are you really doing here?"

Blake poured the chardonnay, handed it to Blank, and

sat down on his favorite chair opposite Blank, who had made himself at home on Blake's sofa.

Blank finally answered. "I just wanted to see how ready you were for Tiffany's appointment with you. And I guess I want to warn Pet about what to expect."

"Please, Blank. I really like Pet. I was just having some recreational sex with Tiff. You know what I mean. Please don't tell Pet."

"No, I don't know what recreational sex is, Blake. I'm married. But it's obvious you intended to bring Tiffany back here, and I wanted so see what kind of wine you drink."

"Actually, I don't drink at all. I just have it here in case a girl, or a lieutenant, gets thirsty."

"Well, you sure are ready for anything. Are we going to find your fingerprints anywhere in Tiffany's car?"

"Yes, I opened her car when she didn't, or couldn't, open it after I drove in."

"How about on her purse when you opened it?"

"What purse?"

"You know, the purse with the words in it. That's going to look funny on the report."

"My prints will not be on her purse, Blank."

"Good to know."

Blake's phone rang, and it was the front gate. Blank identified the caller as Blank's ride. Blake buzzed it in and told Blank his ride was there.

"Nice chatting with you, Blake. I know you didn't kill her. I just have to cover all the bases, right?"

"You bet, Blank. Let me know what you find out, will you? I kind of feel personally involved in this one."

"Sure, Blake. And as usual, you do the same. Remember how we all helped you on the Rocket story? I hope we can count on you too!"

"Of course, Blank. I guess you know the way out."

"Sure do. I'll talk to you soon."

Blank left the condo, and Blake was wondering what Blank meant when he said *we* helped you in kidnapping story. Blake had a funny feeling in his gut but decided it had been a rough day and he may not be thinking clearly. Blake drank his apple cider and went to bed. He wondered what the next day would bring.

14

Blake woke up the next morning at ten o'clock. He needed the sleep. He called his office. "Hi, Liz. Anything going on there?"

"Hi, Blake. The boss really liked your kidnapping story. He's going to submit it for a Pulitzer. But he said that was all in the past, and what do you have for him now?"

"Yeah, that sounds like Rex. I'm working on the murders. Anything else come up to work on?"

"A football player from USC was found dead. Apparently fell from a hundred-and-thirty-foot cliff. The police don't suspect foul play. You want to take it?"

"No, I have enough deaths on my hands. Give it to the beat guy, and let me know if it takes any strange turns."

"Okay. How about an anonymous call from a gal who said one of the Rhinos football players was cheating on his wife?"

"If I wrote about all that's going on, we'd have to start

printing a daily. If it takes a public turn, call me, but I really think that shouldn't get into our magazine unless something bizarre happens."

"Okay," said Liz. "Rex already thinks you act as if you own SRM. How about a UCLA basketball player that was shot in another state?"

"I read about that one. Nothing I can sink my teeth into. I think I'll see what I can do about these murders and see if they're connected. I'm really bummed about Tiffany. I think she was going to tell me something."

"Speaking of girls, a Petula from the sheriff's office wants you to meet her tonight at the Bat Rack at eight o'clock."

"Call her back, will you, Liz? I'm just not up to it tonight."

"She said she won't be near a phone all day. You have to meet her there."

"Who is not near a phone these days? Okay, Liz. See her later."

Blake rested the rest of the day, thinking about yesterday's happenings and building up the courage to face Pet. But at eight sharp, he saw Pet in the lobby of the Bat Rack.

"Well, well, Blake. How are you bloody feeling today?"

"Not great, Pet. Will you give me your cell number so I can get a hold of you in the future?" asked Blake.

"Sure, but I can turn it off when I don't want to be

found. Just like I have it right now. Blank wanted me to see if I can get anything out of you on the murders. Do you have anything?"

"No, I sure don't. Is that why you wanted to meet with me?"

"Of course not. I had to ask to clear my obligation to Blank. Now it's just you and me. Do you like my dress?"

Pet was wearing a so-called basic black dress that was so low-cut it came close to being illegal. It was so short Blake wasn't sure if it was just a top masquerading as a dress. Blake liked it when any woman asked how he liked their dress. He knew full well they meant how did he like what was under it.

"Yeah, I like your dress. It's fantastic. You are really beautiful. And you know it!"

"Yes, I do. And the teasing can stop tonight. Frankly, I want you as much as you want me."

"I was really tired, but I'm getting more awake by the second. Do you want to eat first?"

"No. Let's go to my place."

Pet jumped into Blake's car, and they went to a beautiful home in Spyglass Hill Estates. It was part of a very exclusive part of Newport Beach. Blake was surprised. "How in the world can you live here?"

"Let's just say Daddy is kind to me. Very kind! Let's go in."

"But why do you work with the sheriff's department if your daddy helps you like this?"

"Do you want to ask questions or go up to my heart-shaped bed with the candles already lit?"

Blake chose the bed but was shocked at the furnishings he saw in this house. It had to be five thousand square feet and worth millions. By this time, Pet had stripped down to nothing, and they were both on the heart-shaped bed. Blake could hardly get his clothes off before Pet jumped him. Blake would let the questions go for now. He didn't drink the wine, of course, that was already poured. She did, and he was in heaven.

Blake woke up the next morning and watched Pet serve him breakfast in bed. He was so sore he could hardly adjust the pillows on the heart-shaped bed.

Pet spoke first. "How do you feel, Blake?"

"I feel the best I've ever felt. I'm hungry. But I have to ask, what in the world came over you?"

"There you go with those questions again. Just enjoy. I'm up for seconds. Eat so we can get at it."

It was noon before Blake could finally persuade Pet to put on a robe and accompany him downstairs.

15

"By the way, Pet, anything new on the Cadillac Williams case?"

"What do you know?"

"Just that potassium killed him. But how did he get it?" asked Blake.

"Not sure. Are you going to get something for us?" asked Pet.

There was that *us* again, referring to her position in the sheriff's department.

"I was hoping you had something for *us*, meaning from you to me!" said Blake.

Pet looked at Blake in a way that would melt any man. "You think all of this is to get you to do some investigating for us?"

"Well, sometimes I think ..."

"Sometimes you think too much, Blake. Nobody bloody makes me do anything. And by the way, *us* includes the sheriff's department, including me!"

"You're right, Pet. You certainly are your own person. I think the killer is probably Doc Strogham. I'll talk to him and let you know what I find."

"Why do you suspect him?" asked Pet.

"I think he was upset that his son, Kyle, was delegated to second string. It will mean a lot at contract time."

"If you can sneak anything out of his doctor's bag, that would be great too. We don't have concrete probable cause to do anything yet, but you are an investigative reporter, not a cop. We can use everything you get," said Pet.

"Okay, Pet. But I gotta go before I fall dead right on your heart-shaped bed. Talk to you soon."

Blake again marveled at the house he was leaving and knew there was a lot to know about Pet. He would make it a point to find that out, but he knew it would have to be on Pet's terms.

Blake also knew that Doc would be at the stadium today, as some of the players were coming in for year-round exercise. He drove to Orange Grove Stadium and found Doc with a clipboard in his hand.

"Hey, Doc, what's new?"

"Nothing at all. Just supervising some workouts today."

"And fans think football is a six-month sport!"

"Yeah, it's definitely a year-round sport with the drafts, trades, conditioning, hiring, and firings. Even twelve months isn't enough."

"Say, Doc, Cadillac was found with a large dose of potassium in his system. That killed him. Any idea how he got that?"

"Hey, scribe, are you trying to pin this on me?"

"I'm not the police. I don't pin. It's just that you had been seen giving Cadillac a lot of injections for weeks before—"

"I told you before I was giving him B_{12}. Remember?"

"I know what you told me, but I'm cynical by nature. If that rock don't roll, I can't sleep. Can I see one of those syringes?"

"Okay, okay, you got me. I was giving him steroids. He wanted 'em, and I gave it to him. But I would never kill anyone!"

Blake looked at Doc with a pretend look of understanding. "Your son benefited from all of this. Now he's back to number one and negotiating a new contract that will be twice as big as a backup would get. But I understand, you have to protect your son."

Doc looked at Blake, pleading with him to believe him. "I would never give poison to a ballplayer. I'm here to help them. They trust me. You know what a trainer is to them; they're all like my sons!"

"Give me a syringe with the steroids in them," said Blake, knowing it was probably way too late for any evidence to be available, but he did promise Pet.

"Uh, I don't have any. I have to get a new source. My

source dried up. Tiffany was getting the steroids for me, and now that she's gone, I have to find someone else. Or maybe I can get these guys to quit. I'm just in the air right now."

"Are you telling me you got the steroids from Tiffany? The same Tiffany that was just shot to death?"

"That's right. She's a cheerleader here, or was, and maybe she was just a messenger. I don't know, Blake. I just got them from her and paid her cash. But I didn't kill Cadillac or anyone else. You have to believe me!"

"I don't know what to believe. I'm stunned. You better not be lying about Tiffany!"

"Why would I lie about Tiffany? I don't want to get her into trouble; I'm just trying to come clean with you. I didn't kill ..."

Blake stopped listening. Tiffany supplying steroids? It wasn't really a big issue, considering he was investigating two murders, but Blake couldn't concentrate on anything Doc told him now. "I'll be back to see you. You can bet on that."

Blake walked out of the stadium and right past gate 7, where Tiffany had been found dead in her car. Was there a tie-in with Cadillac's murder? Was Tiffany a drug runner?

16

The next morning, Blake was awakened by the ring on his cell phone. "Hi, Liz. What time is it?"

Liz said it was eleven o'clock and that Rex Harrington wanted to meet him for lunch at the Bat Rack at noon. Blake agreed and met Rex there at noon.

"You look like shit, Blake," said Rex. "Must have had a good night, huh?"

"No, it wasn't. I just can't figure all of this out. First, Cadillac is murdered. Then Tiffany the cheerleader is killed. I don't know if there is a tie-in or not, and then I find out that Tiffany might have been running steroids to Doc Strogham for use by the Rhinos football team. She would never do that. I just can't believe that."

"Could you believe it if you weren't, uh, involved with her? Are you being really objective about this?" asked Rex.

"I wasn't really involved with her. We had good times,

but I just can't believe she was supplying drugs to the Rhinos, and I can't believe she is dead."

"Perhaps there is more to this, Blake. Perhaps the drugs were tied into her murder. How does Doc fit into all of this?"

"I still think he had the motive and the means to kill Cadillac. He could have given him the potassium easy as shit. But he sure is a good actor if he's guilty. Or maybe I'm just in shock about him implicating Tiff. I'm just not sure right now."

"Maybe you need a rest, Blake. Maybe it's time to divert your attention to clear your head."

Blake was astonished. "You want me to take a vacation? You?"

"No, of course not. You know publishers think that writing about sports is vacation enough. I was thinking of another story. We got word Rameesh Lewis is getting worse in the hospital. They won't let anyone see him."

"Wait a minute. You're talking about the professional basketball player who went into a rest home after a nervous breakdown?"

"That's the guy. He's in Green Briar in Garden Grove. His agent said he was so drugged he didn't make sense, and now they say he's so bad no one is even allowed to visit him. And by the way, we could use a few more stories from you while you're working on the Cadillac and

Tiffany story. That's the business, you know. It could take you some time to figure out those."

"Okay, I'll look into it, but I'm not quitting until I know what happened to Cadillac and Tiffany."

"No one is asking you to quit that. Just see if you can find out what happened to Lewis. It'll make a great story."

"All right, all right. But right now I'm going back to bed to try to clear my head."

Blake said goodbye to his boss and headed home. As he was driving home, his pants pocket vibrated. It was Pet. "Hi, Blake. Did you get anything out of Doc Strogham?"

"Well, he said he was just giving Cadillac steroids. I hope that doesn't mean you guys will arrest him."

"No, we'll pinch that bird for murder. I agree with you he did the deed. Did you get us a vile of his steroids?"

"No, I didn't. And he wouldn't still have potassium by now. Why don't you have your guys talk to him and see what he says?"

"Maybe. But you found out a lot. Anything else?"

"No, that was about it. What are you doing tonight? I want to see that great house of yours again, Pet."

"Sure, Blake. Come on by at seven, and I'll make us some veal cutlets. But you better be looking at more than my home."

"Pet, to be truthful, when you're in the room, I don't see anything else."

"That was the right thing to say, Blake. See you at seven."

Blake completed his drive home and took a long nap. He would need it to keep up with Pet.

17

The trip from Blake's Newport Beach home to Spyglass Hill wasn't far, but Blake had to be cleared by the gateman before he could enter the estates. Blake still couldn't believe Pet could live in such an expensive home. He walked up the long sidewalk to her home and rang the bell. Pet answered the door.

"Hi, Pet. Your favorite sports reporter is here."

"Hi, Blake. Do you like my leopard lounging pajamas?"

Blake looked at Pet in her form-fitting pajamas, and she had a form that was nice to fit. It was so low-cut some would say she was topless. "Yes, it's great. I like the latest fashions!" What else could Blake say?

"Come have veal, Blake. Do you like meatballs?"

"I'm all for meatballs. Let's eat."

Blake and Pet sat down at a very romantically set table, complete with candles and two chairs almost on top of each other. Pet poured wine for herself and grape juice for Blake.

The meal didn't last long, as the two were on the heart-shaped bed, going at it hot and heavy. About an hour later, the two were sitting up, holding each other's hand.

"Say, Pet. I want to really thank you for the information on Rocket Wallace. My editor put it up for a Pulitzer Prize. That would really be something for me."

"You're welcome, Blake. By the way, that article has already been published, right?"

"Oh yes. SRM is a weekly magazine. We put that out two weeks ago. It was a big success."

"I've been feeling guilty about something."

"What? Is the story not true? I talked to a dentist and everything."

"No, almost everything is true—except one thing. But you have to promise me not to publish this, and never tell anyone where you got the information."

Blake had a burning sensation in his stomach. What in the world was Pet going to say? Blake didn't respond to her off-the-record request but just stared at her.

Pet continued. "The GPS was in his body. Not his tooth. I just can't stand lying to you, but Blank made me do it. He said it would be putting the lives of many people in danger if it was published."

"I can see that. But I thought the tooth technology was really something. Why even tell me that?"

"The information on the tooth plant was leaked to

enough people that Blank thought it would come out soon anyway. He wanted you to have the story first. He was thinking of you. So was I. And by the way, there have been many tooth-implant GPS's in celebrities."

"Great. I mean, thank you. But I wrote something that wasn't true, or at least the body part of the GPS wasn't true. But I talked to that dentist guy, and how about Dr. Garmin? They were all lying?"

"Actually, no. We told them about the tooth plant and didn't tell them not to tell anyone unless it became known. We knew you would say it was okay, and you got it from us. We just wanted to end it right there. I really didn't think it would harm you, Blake."

"I just don't like to write something that's not true. I know I use some questionable tactics, and I even lie too, but I don't like to publish anything that's not true."

"Everything's true, Blake. Just the placement of the GPS. You just can't print the new truth now."

"What is the truth?"

Pet looked pensive but not entirely sad about the revelation. "As you know, the computer chips are getting smaller and smaller. Just look at how small computers are. You can hold them in your hand.

"Anyway, surgeons can put these GPS chips just anywhere in the body. The problem of rejection has been worked out in most parts of the body. The best place right now is in a big artery. The GPS looks like a stent that keeps arteries open."

"Why do they put stents in when they can put it in a tooth?"

"Some of our kidnappers have knocked out every tooth in some of their captives. What would they do if they knew about this? Or even the possibility of putting a GPS in other parts of the body?"

"Yeah, I see what you mean. And if I write a retraction, I'm spilling the beans. I'm in a quandary here, Pet."

"Not really. Just leave the story as is. Everyone's forgotten about it by now anyway."

"I know it, Pet. I know it! I don't know what I'm going to do, but please never do that again. I'd rather take a *no comment* than face this."

"No problem, Blake. Now let's go for another round."

"I'm not in the mood, Pet. Don't take this wrong. You did help, and I'm not eternally pissed. It's just I have to figure what to do next. I think I can do that in my bed better than yours. Please don't take this wrong. It must have been hard on you to tell me about it."

"Yes, it did, Blake. You mean more to me than that. At least you do now. That's why I told you. By the way, I like your hard part."

Blake got up, dressed, and went home to Newport Bay in Newport Beach. He had a lot to think about.

18

Blake was at his office early the next morning, talking to SRM's editor in chief, Rex Harrington. "Rex, I think part of my story on the GPS in Rocket Wallace isn't holding up. It seems I was duped on the placement of the GPS."

"Did you have more than one source?"

"I had four sources. The dentist, the GPS manufacturer, and two police officials confirmed it."

"And how many sources now say something different?"

"Well, just one. Lt. Blank Smith's so-called secretary."

"Was she one of the original alleged liars?"

"Well, yes, she was. I think she was playing me the first time but not now."

Blake gazed at Rex with a puzzled look. "I think she is now telling the truth."

"Well, Blake, as you know, I already submitted that story for a Pulitzer. The story is all true except for the placement of the GPS, and even that correction was given to you by a previous liar. I think we should leave it alone. If in the future we have to, we'll run a correction on page 20. I don't want you to waste any more time on this. You have two murders and a nut farm to investigate. That's enough."

"I understand, Rex. I guess I have played so many people I'm just not used to being played. I'll drop it for now."

"Good. I need a story from you soon. Get on that Rameesh story and get something in so the readers don't forget who you are."

"Okay, Rex. I'll get on it."

Blake walked down the long corridor back to his office and stopped at Liz's desk on the way.

"Hi, Liz. Any calls?"

"Nah. With cell phones these days, there are a lot fewer calls to me. We have gotten a lot of letters complimenting you on the GPS story."

"That's great. But now I have to go to a rest home."

"Good. You need the rest," said Liz, smirking.

"No, not for me. Can you get me some information on Green Briar in Garden Grove?"

"Already got it. It's a place where celebrities and rich people go for a rest. Some have had nervous breakdowns, and others have had mental problems. Others go suffering from exhaustion. I couldn't get confirmation that Rameesh Wallace was in the place."

"Great. Sounds like a tough case. I guess it is possible he's in there for a rest and just doesn't want anyone snooping around."

"His agent, Sam Klein, thinks something's up. Here is his telephone number."

"Thanks, Liz. Great job. I'll be in touch."

Blake went into his office and called Sam Klein. Klein's secretary put him right through. "Thank goodness someone is listening. Even if it's just a reporter," Klein said.

"Well, I'm talking to just an attorney. Have you talked to the cops?" asked Blake.

"Yes, but they said they need more than I can give them to open a case. My investigator struck out too."

"What is it you suspect?"

"I don't really know. Rameesh went in there because he was exhausted from the pressure of playing pro basketball, and maybe a little depression from his divorce and his parents being killed in a fire. He's been in there a month, and all of a sudden, he's a blithering idiot. He just stares at me and can hardly talk. Actually, now they won't even let me see him."

"I'll see what I can dig up. Let me know if you hear anything. I'll have Liz email you my numbers. Of course, I get exclusives rights? Thanks."

Blake hung up the phone and walked out of the office with a lot on his mind. He didn't even say goodbye to Liz. Blake decided to drive to Garden Grove and visit the Green Briar.

Blake pulled into a very long driveway that led to what looked like a colonial home. In fact, it looked just like a southern mansion surrounded by eucalyptus trees. It had a very peaceful and secluded ambiance. It was easy to see why movie stars and other celebrities liked this place.

Blake walked up the stairs and entered a lobby filled with antique chairs and couches. It looked like something out of *Gone with the Wind*. The lobby was completely empty. That seemed odd. Blake walked up to a closed window and rang a buzzer. It took about two minutes for a woman, not bad-looking but not great-looking either, to answer the buzzer and open a window. "Yes, what can I do for you?"

"Good morning. I'm from *Sports Register* Magazine. I'm here to interview Rameesh Wallace. We're doing a piece on injured or incapacitated athletes. Where can I find him?"

"I'm Linda. Does Dr. Tortolano know you are coming today?"

"He should. My secretary said she made an appointment."

"Well, I have to check with Dr. Tortolano. Please have a seat."

Blake sat on one of the chairs and waited a half hour

for her return. Blake was trying to remember where he heard that name. He still couldn't figure it out when Linda finally came back.

"Dr. Tortolano said he never talked to your office, and Mr. Wallace is way too sick to speak to you. Sorry."

"Then tell Dr. Tortolano I will speak to him. I'm not leaving until I do."

Blake waited about an hour. Only one person came in during that hour. That visitor had an appointment. *Guess that's part of the security promised to celebs*, thought Blake.

Finally, Dr. Tortolano came out. Blake stood and extended his hand. Dr. Tortolano did not shake it and sat down next to him. Blake sat back down. "What can I do for you?"

"I'm doing story on—"

"Yes, yes, I know. But Rameesh Wallace is too sick to be interviewed. Linda told you that."

"Yes, but there is some concern about his health. He has a lot of fans. What can I tell them?"

"Tell them he is fine. He's just here for some rest. Part of his problem was putting up with reporters like you. Give him some privacy."

"What problems does he have?"

"You know I can't discuss that with you. Now, I would like you to leave. Give me your card, and I'll call you when he can speak with you."

"I really just want to see him for a few short minutes. He owes that to his fans." Blake handed the doctor his card.

"You are wearing my patience very thin. What is your name?"

"Blake Brennon. It's on my card."

"You are not going to see him now. I must ask that you leave the premises."

"Okay, but if I don't see him soon, I'll have to write that it's strange that even his own agent isn't allowed to see him. This could blow up into a big scandal."

"Be careful, Mr. Brennon. When things *blow up*, people get injured. Some innocent, some not so innocent."

"I'll be back soon, Dr. Tortolano. Very soon. The fans have a right to know!" Blake thought, *That rock don't roll!*

Blake turned his back on Dr. Tortolano, and a cold sweat developed on his neck. Blake got in his car and dialed his cell phone. "Liz, get me everything you can on this Dr. Anthony Tortolano. This guy is like something out of the *Godfather* movie."

Liz replied, "That's funny. He's got the same name that was on Tiffany's note found in her purse. Oh well. I'll get some info on him."

Blake closed the phone and saw Dr. Tortolano looking at him from his second-story office. Blake thought, *Yes, that's where I remember that name. It was on that paper I found in Tiff's purse the night she was murdered.*

It's probably just a coincidence. Blake looked back at Tortolano still looking at him from his window and said out loud to himself, "I'll see you real soon, Dr. Tortolano. Real soon!"

Blake drove out of the parking lot onto Garden Grove Boulevard to contemplate his next move.

19

Two days later, Blake went back to his office and talked to Liz. "Do you have anything for me on Tortolano?"

"Yes, but I was told not to give it to you until you fill out your parking pass renewal."

"Come on, Liz, give me the info. I'll do it later."

"I filled it out for you. Just sign at the bottom."

Blake signed his name without reading the parking form, gave it back to Liz, and yelled, "Now please give me the Tortolano stuff!"

"Before I do that, here is an email from Mr. Klein, Rameesh's agent."

Blake looked over the email. It contained the name and address and telephone number of Rameesh's ex-wife and other people connected with the basketball team. Blake would follow up on it later.

"Now, Liz. Now! I want Tortolano's file!"

"Okay, hold your horses," teased Liz. "Here it is."

Blake grabbed the file and made his way into his office while reading the file. Dr. Tortolano had investigations for malpractice and falsifying documents for his patients but no convictions. On paper, he was okay, but why did he treat Blake like he did, and why was he hiding Rameesh?"

Blake put in a call to Lt. Blank Smith. "Blank, do you know anything about Anthony Tortolano over at Green Briar?"

"Well, hello to you too. Am I now your humble servant?"

"Sorry, Blank. I've got a lot on my mind. His agent said Rameesh Wallace went in Green Briar for a rest, and his agent says he talks like a zombie. And Dr. Tortolano treats me like a pariah. Know anything?"

"I can't imagine anyone not wanting to welcome you into their lives with open arms, Blake. But this guy Tortolano is a funny guy. He doesn't like his integrity threatened. A few people have called about improper treatment by Tortolano, and others have complained about the quantity of medications prescribed, but I've always referred them to the medical board. They handle medical complaints."

"Do you have the medical board's number?"

"You don't need it, Blake. Every complaint on doctors is listed on the internet. If it's not official, no one talks."

"Isn't that like the fox guarding the henhouse? Blank?"

"You mean like police investigating police, or lawyers investigating lawyers? And by the way, who investigates you guys?"

"The public investigates us," Blake said, trying not to laugh. "Anything more on this guy?"

"Several people have called and said the good doctor has tried to intimidate them by saying he would keep their family members in for longer periods of time if they complained to anyone. But again, this is really a matter for the medical board."

"Can he keep them? Can't they just check out?"

"Some got in there on a 5150 from police and mental illness practitioners. If Tortolano says they are a danger to themselves or others, he can keep them longer than the original seventy-two hours. Some family members are glad to have some of the patients out of their hair. It's very hard to deal with some troubled people."

"But most of the patients there are wealthy, even celebrities, right?"

"Sure. In that case, the families get guardianship or conservatory edicts from the courts and hope Grandpa stays there while they spend his money."

"You are more cynical than I am. But I get your drift."

"Let me know if you get anything on this guy I can use, Blake. It isn't like I haven't been trying to get him for years; I just don't like his attitude. I'd love to bust him for something."

"I'll certainly let you know. Take care, Blank." Blake hung up the phone and decided to take a drive to see if he could visit Rameesh's ex-wife, Patricia.

Blake drove to Brea, a city in the northernmost part of Orange County. The house was okay but not what Blake expected for the ex-wife of a major basketball star. Blake went up the short walk to her front door. A beleaguered African American woman answered the door with a bunch of kids playing in the background. She looked like she could be beautiful after three days of rest and some makeup. "Patricia?" Blake never called a divorcee by her prior married name. Some took offense to that.

"Yes, I'm Pat. What do you want? I'm not buying nothing."

"I'm not selling. I just wondered if I could talk to you about Rameesh."

"I haven't heard from the bastard for over two months. Do you know where he is?"

"Yes, I do. Can we sit down?"

"Yes, I guess it's safe. You are not going to do much to me with four kids hanging around."

Blake didn't quite get the logic, but he entered a standard living room cluttered with toys and clothes. Blake picked up a Batman doll and a Batmobile and sat on the edge of the sofa, while Patricia made no attempt to help. She sat on the large chair that looked like it was made for Rameesh. Patricia's legs didn't come close to the floor.

"Where is he?" asked Patricia.

"He is in Green Briar. Don't you read the newspapers?"

"What is Green Briar? And do you think I have time to read newspapers? I did read he was exhausted. Poor baby. I really don't feel sorry for him. Hey, Jordan, stop picking on LaBron! Sorry about that."

"That's okay. Green Briar is a rest home. Some people call it a sanitarium. He's apparently in pretty bad shape."

"Let me know if he croaks. Maybe then I'll get what's due me."

"Well, we'll see about that. Can you tell me anything about him?"

"He used to be an okay guy. Then he started to use and drink. He became a different person. Now he doesn't see his kids and pays me very little. He told me when he dies, I will get a million dollars. Hopefully that's sooner than later. I think he was shaving points too. A lot of strange people visited us when we were together in Laguna Hills. Now that was a house!"

"Shaving points? In basketball games? Does that really happen?" asked Blake.

"Boy, I thought you were a sports reporter. Sure it happens. Las Vegas makes a spread. Let's say the Lakers by ten. The Lakers can still win, but if they win by only nine or less, the money winner is the other team's better. Get it?"

"I know what point-shaving is," said a disturbed Blake. "I just didn't think it happened anymore."

"Man, you are dense. Anything with that much money involved, there's always going to be shenanigans. Now I'm not 100 percent sure Rameesh was doing it. Don't quote me."

"No, I'm not going to quote you. I don't even think it has anything to do with his stay at Green Briar. I'm just shocked to think that point-shaving still exists."

"Michael, put Jordan down right now," yelled Patricia. "Listen, Blake, is it? I have to go. My kids are killing each other. Call me if you know when I can reach him. I need money!"

"I will. Good luck, Pat." Blake found the door himself as Patricia raced into the playroom. He didn't get much information, but he might look into the point-shaving thing later. Right now, he had two murders and the Rameesh thing to look into. Blake got back into his BMW and back on the 57 freeway toward Newport. Blake stopped at the Bat Rack to get a soda and think.

20

Just as he sat down, his cell phone rang. It was Liz. "Hi, Blake. Do you know a guy by the name of Brian Anderson?"

"Sure. He's an old friend of my dad's. Brian coached with George Allen, Tom Landry, and a couple of other guys. He's been in about five Super Bowls as a coach in the NFL."

"Make that six, Blake. He has six Super Bowl rings. Or should I say he *had* six Super Bowl rings."

"What do you mean had?"

"He was mugged in Westminster, and the rings were stolen."

"Why in the world was he carrying six Super Bowl rings?"

"Do you want me to write this story for you too?"

"I'm really busy. Call Anderson and tell him to call the police."

"Actually, it wasn't Brian who called. It was your dad. He asked if you could do him a favor and help find the rings."

"Oh boy. How do I say no to Dad? I love Dad, but I've got so much going on."

"I'll email you Brian's info. And you tell Brian to report this to the police. Call him! Rex likes the story idea too. He says we need something from you for next week."

"Okay, Liz. Send it over. As if I don't have enough going right now. Bye."

Blake thought about his dad, Hubert Brennon. Hubert played football for Phoenix Junior College and played quarterback in the Junior College Rose Bowl in Pasadena. Hubert coached football at the high school level and a short stint at Los Angeles Community College before retiring recently.

Blake tried to see his mother and father as much as he could, but his business took up a lot of his time. They lived in Culver City, about one hour from Orange County, which meant by the time he got back to Orange County, most of the day was shot. But at least now Blake's parents didn't work, so they could be seen on Blake's so-called weekend of Mondays and Tuesdays.

Blake looked at his iPhone and saw the information Liz promised to send. Blake thought to himself, *how can I look for rings when a man is hidden in an asylum and two people are dead?*

Blake thought maybe the ring story could be wrapped

up quickly. He decided to call Brian. "Hi, Brian. I heard you got robbed!"

"Yes, sir. I was coming home from an interview at Spectrum Cable, and I was jumped by four hooded, young, strong, muscular guys."

"How do you know they were young?"

"If they weren't, I could've taken them. There were only four. Heck, I took on bigger guys than that when I played college ball."

Blake believed the young Brian could have taken on four guys in the old days, but now Brian was in his seventies with bum knees, and his back was ailing. "Brian, what were you doing with all six Super Bowl rings in your possession?"

"I was interviewed on a Spectrum cable show called 'Talking Sports.' I got in my car, drove a couple of miles to my apartment, and four guys jumped me outside my apartment. They only took my rings!"

"But they are worth a lot of money, especially to collectors. Did you call the police?"

"Yeah, they said murders and bodily injury stuff have a higher priority. Maybe you can talk to them and tell them how important these rings are. They really represent my life."

"I know that, Brian. I'll see what I can do. In the meantime, think about anything you can remember about the incident. By the way, are you hurt?"

"Naw. They just pushed me down. I got hurt worse on the football field every Saturday, I can tell you that! I'll start thinking of what they said, but I don't think it was anything but 'cooperate or die.' I didn't cooperate. I guess I'm lucky they didn't kill me."

"By the way, Brian, how did they know you had the rings on you?"

"I don't know. The show was taped for a later airing, so I just can't figure it out."

"Okay. I'll see what I can do. Go rest, and I'll be in touch." Blake closed his cell phone and knew why people got drunk. He considered starting drinking right then but decided against it. *Murders, point-shaving, a player in an asylum, and now Super Bowl rings. What's next?*

21

Blake decided to drive to the Spectrum studio in Garden Grove where the show was taped. Blake parked and entered the building. He was surprised to see three receptionists behind heavy glass windows, similar to the setup of banks in some urban towns.

Blake spoke through a hole in the glass. "I'm here to see the producer of a cable show called 'Talking Sports.'"

"Do you have an appointment?" asked a young lady about one hundred pounds overweight, with a microphone on her end.

"No, but it's important. What's the producer's name?"

"Wait here, and I'll see if Michael Borack can see you. What is this regarding?"

"It's about a recent guest that almost lost his life."

The lady didn't respond and put on an earphone. Blake couldn't make out what she was saying, but she came back and ordered Blake to sign the guest book and said Michael would be right out.

About five minutes later, a man, about forty and wearing a T-shirt, came out to greet Blake. "Come on in. I will escort you back to my office."

The two walked back through some cubicles and entered Michael's little office. Blake could tell Michael was a real sports fan, with many pictures and sports memorabilia decorating his already too small office. Michael spoke first. "What's this about some guy getting hurt?"

Blake knew Brian wasn't really hurt, but he had to get Michael's attention. "Yes, you had a Brian Anderson on the show recently?"

"Try just last week. The guy with the Super Bowl rings. What happened to him?"

"He was mugged, and the rings were stolen. He's okay, but those rings meant a lot to him."

"His show is going to air next week. Do you want me to stop it?"

"No, I just need to know everyone who knew he was going to be on the show."

"The only people who knew were Don and Jim, the hosts, as well as the camera crew. About ten people. When did the mugging take place?"

"On his way home from here. Same day. About eleven thirty."

"We were all here. It takes at least an hour to break everything down. Why are you asking these questions?"

"It appears that someone knew he would be carrying the rings home. That's all they stole. Just his rings! I need a list of—"

"Of course. I can write it right now for you." Michael Borack wrote the list of eight names and handed it to Blake. The list omitted Michael's name, but Blake added it.

"Can I see the tape of the interview?" asked Blake.

"Sure, but it's not edited yet. Do you want to see the raw footage?"

"Yes, that would be even better."

Michael took Blake to the editing room and ran the tape. There was nothing out of the ordinary, just the two guys interviewing Brian about his days as a player, coach and the Super Bowls.

Blake thanked Michael for his troubles and was escorted back to the lobby. Blake forgot to ask Michael about the reason for the security. Perhaps another day. Blake walked out to his car, wishing he didn't have the rings to think about.

Blake called Liz to see about messages.

"Blake, why can't you just give out your cell phone number?"

"I'm a busy man. Can't handle all of those calls. That's why I have you, Liz."

"Great. Your dad called to see if you found the guy who stole the rings, and Rameesh's agent called in a panic. In addition, Blank called to see if you know anything else on the murders."

"Tell them all I'm going on vacation! Bye." Blake hung up to really contemplate a vacation. *Yeah, right!* Blake called Sam Klein first.

"Hi, Sam. Anything new on Rameesh?"

"No. I'm trying to get a court order to see him, but if he's like he was the last time I saw him, it won't do any good. Is there anything you can do outside of the legal system to see him?"

"I'll see what I can do. But it may just be he's had a breakdown."

"I don't believe it for a second. Please see what you can do. I'll give you all the scoops from my office for a decade."

"I will, I will. Talk to you later."

Blake drove home where he could think. He opened his front door, and there was Pet. She sat seductively on his couch, wearing a black miniskirt, red panties, and a see-through white blouse, no bra. If there was a sexier woman in this universe, it would have to be her twin. "How did you get in … never mind."

"Hi, Blake. How was your day?"

"Just peachy. Do you know anyone in the Westminster Police Department?"

"Sure, the sheriff's department knows all of the local law enforcement. What do you need?"

"I just need a quick resolution to a mugging case down there. I really need to get back to the murders and another case I'm working on."

"I'll call someone down there tomorrow. Now come over here, and I'll rub your neck."

Blake sat down next to Pet on the couch, and she commenced rubbing his neck. She didn't rub it very hard, but Blake loved every minute of it. "By the way, why are you here?"

"Blank asked me to give you the latest on the murders and to see if you know anything."

"You go first."

"Fine. We interviewed Doc. He has a motive and the means. We just don't have any proof. Blank wants you to grind him. Will you do that? Ever since law enforcement lost our hot spotlight and that Miranda case, it's been tough," said Pet with a smirk.

"Yeah, I was going to talk to him anyway. Does Blank think Tiffany's murder is connected?"

"To be honest, Blake, we don't have a thing on that one. She was going to meet you, and that was the last thing she did before you found her. The only suspect would be you. But we know you are innocent. It would be nice to find someone else we could pin that one on. Now, what do you have?"

"Nothing at all. My boss has me chasing rings and mental asylums. But I will start again on that soon."

"Good. Now take off your bloody clothes and tell me how the autopsy went."

"You Brits have a way with words, especially after watching an autopsy. Let me take a shower, eat a sandwich. You drink some wine, and I'll be back"

Blake decided to eat a sandwich first, as Pet had already eaten. He went into the bathroom, disrobed, and got into his stall shower. It wasn't thirty seconds before Pet, sans her miniskirt and everything else, was standing next to him. Blake was thinking this day might end on a high note after all.

The two took foreplay to a new high, and it ended on Blake's bed with both of them soaking wet. They never did use towels, as eventually they both fell into a deep sleep.

Blake awoke the next morning to the smell of hot coffee and bacon and eggs. Pet sure had a lot of energy, he thought. Blake got up, put a robe on, and saw Pet in one of his T-shirts. "No man's fantasy can be this good. Good morning, Pet."

"And a good morning to you, Blake. Have some breakfast. Then I have to scoot. I have to report to Blank this morning. After that, I'll call the Westminster PD."

"I hope you don't have to report everything to Blank," said Blake.

"No. I don't put in for overtime when I'm with you. I'm here because I want to be."

"Me too," said Blake, not knowing how to answer her. "Let's get dressed and start the day. Who knows? Maybe something will break today."

Pet left, and Blake showered again. This time was not nearly the adventure of last night, but he had work to do. Pet went to the sheriff's station.

Just before Blake left, his home phone rang. It was Pet. "Hi, Blake. Still in bed? Anyway, I talked to Captain Baines at the WMPD, and he said he wants to see you. Now would be a good time."

"Thanks, Pet. I'll go right over. Anything new from Blank?"

"Haven't seen him yet. I wanted to get this to you. I hope he helps you. Baines is a good guy. Bye."

Blake put on his sports jacket and headed to the Westminster Police Department.

22

B lake parked at the Westminster courthouse and walked across the courtyard to the police department. He walked in and asked for Captain Baines. A beautiful redhead at the front desk flirtatiously asked Blake if he had an appointment. Blake was thinking that all the receptionists at the police departments were really looking good lately.

"Yes, I do. It was set up by Petula at the sheriff's department."

The redhead called back, and a stout-looking man in his fifties walked toward Blake. It was Captain Baines. "Come on in, Mr. Brennon."

The two walked back to a small office. Blake sat in the chair, while Captain Baines sat behind his desk.

"I'll be blunt, Mr. Brennon. I think Brian Anderson set the whole thing up. I don't think there were four robbers, no robbery. He made it all up. His story changed several times in one interview."

"What? He would never do that. I've known him for years."

"He's hurting financially. Last year, he insured the rings for their market value, averaging fifteen thousand dollars each. The insurance company is about ready to pay off."

"But those rings are worth much more than that to football fans."

"I'm well aware, but under a normal policy, he can only get what the diamonds and gold add up to. If he went to Lloyds of London or the likes, he could have insured them for more."

"But he was mugged. Four guys in hoods—"

"Yeah, four guys in hoods. Not one guy, not two, but four. He said several times that it would take four guys to get those rings because he's tough! He described all of them the same. Identical. In our second interview, he said one guy had a Mexican accent. In the first interview, he said it sounded Oriental."

"But, Captain Baines, I've known this guy for years. He is a friend of my father's. I just can't believe this."

"We're going to arrest him in the next couple of days for insurance fraud and filing a false police report. It would go better for him if he turned himself in. A lot better. The only reason I'll give him a break is because I love your stuff in SRM. How come you guys don't have a swimsuit edition?"

"I don't know, Captain. Thanks for reading my work. Let me snoop around a bit. Please don't arrest him until you hear from me, okay?"

"A couple of days, Mr. Brennon. I'll wait that long. I'm notifying the insurance company today."

"Please hold off on that too, aside from the delay in payment. Let me see what I can find."

Blake left the captain's office in a daze. He had to prove that Brian was really mugged. But now even he doubted Brian's story. There was a knot starting to grow in Blake's stomach. Blake got into his car and immediately made a beeline to Brian's apartment. On the way, he called his dad on his cell. "Hi, Dad. Has Brian called you?"

"No, but he dropped by yesterday with some boxes. He asked me to keep them here. Not enough room at his apartment."

"Dad, please open those boxes right away. I'll hold while you do that."

"Son, I can't open those boxes. That would violate his privacy. I've known him for—"

"Please, Dad, you could be saving him a long time in prison. Open them now and tell me what you find."

"Okay, Blake, but later you gotta fill me in. Hold on."

Blake pulled up to Brian's apartment complex and waited for about five minutes before his dad finally came back to the phone. "Blake, I can't believe this. The six Super Bowl rings are here in the same little box I've always seen them in. This box was in the big box. What is going on?"

"I'll tell you later, Dad. Keep them there for now. I'll get back to you."

Blake didn't even say goodbye as he shut his iPhone off. He walked up to Brian's first-floor apartment and rang the doorbell. Brian answered.

"Well, Blake. It's great to see you again. Come on in! How about some coffee?"

"No thanks, Brian. How about going over that mugging again for me."

"Not right now, Blake. I'm kinda tired."

"How are things financially?" Blake asked as he sat on a chair.

"Not great. Pensions for coaches and players were practically nonexistent when I coached and played, and the wages weren't even a fraction of what they are now. You know that today some head pro football coaches are paid over ten million a year?"

"I'm well aware of that, Brian. Sportswriters aren't keeping up either. It's a shame you lost those valuable Super Bowl rings."

Brian looked down. A tear came from his right eye. "You know, don't you?"

"Yes, I know, and so do the police. And Dad knows too. That rock really don't roll!"

"Can we keep this quiet? I really need the money."

"It's a cat that's left the bag. Here's what I suggest. First, you call the insurance company and tell them you found the rings and to cancel the claim. You haven't taken any money yet, so I think you'll be all right there. Second, you call Captain Baines and tell him you're coming in. You do that now, and you go in now. Then you call Dad and tell him you will pick up the rings at his house. You have to tell him what you did."

Blake felt sorry for Brian. He always thought of him as a great coach and a man with a lot of pride. Blake knew this was hard on him, but at the same time, he knew his dad would be very hurt by all of this. Blake was angry too.

"I just can't do all of this, Blake. I can't face your dad. I can't go to jail with those criminals I've always detested," said Brian.

"Brian, you may not go to jail. Or if you do, it might be a very short stay. After that, I'll help you with some social service contacts."

"You mean charity?" asked Brian.

"Just some help. You need some help. Don't let your pride get in the way."

"You think this is just pride? I've never done something like this, Blake. Honest."

"I believe you, Brian. Now you have work to do. I gotta go." Blake left and walked back to his car. He thought of calling his dad but decided to let Brian do his own dirty work. Blake drove off to Green Briar in Garden Grove.

23

Green Briar was just a few miles from Westminster, so Blake got there in ten minutes. He drove up and walked in. The receptionist was typing a form and was startled by Blake's presence. "You again. Mr. Barton, is it?"

"No, Brennon. I'm here to see Rameesh Lewis. Is he in?"

"Visits by relatives have to be approved by Dr. Tortolano. Are you a relative? Before you answer, I know he is black and you are white and you write for some magazine."

"That kinda narrows down my options—Lydia, is it?"

"You see my name on my badge in big letters, Mr. Barton. Linda. What do you want?"

Before Blake could answer, Dr. Tortolano came out with a couple of Bubbas—Blake's term for enforcers and big football players.

"You cannot interview Mr. Lewis. He is not in any condition to talk to you. What part of go away and stay away don't you understand?"

"Fans want to know about him. What can you tell me?"

"As I said before, Mr. Brennon, I cannot give out that information. Now I must insist that you leave."

"I'll be back. Maybe I can match your Bubbas with my Bubbas. Then we'd have a standoff."

"You better bring more Bubbas than that. I have a hospital full of them. Now get out of here."

Blake left and thought about the many athletes he'd talked to doctors about. They all gave out information called condition reports. Sure this was a mental thing, but why all the secrecy? Blake drove out and stopped at Tommy's for a chili dog.

Tommy's was a famous eatery known for their greasy, great chili. Tommy's was copied all over the Los Angeles–Orange County area with names like Tomy's and Tom's. But there was only one Tommy's with their seven locations in the several counties. Blake consumed his chili dog and decided to head to his office. He knew he had to smoke Tortolano out, but how was another matter.

Blake caught up on some paperwork and told Rex a story on the Super Bowl rings was coming very soon. How was he going to write such a story? Blake felt really torn, so he went home. After dinner, he called his dad.

"Hi, Dad. How's Mom? Good. Did, ah, Brian call you? No? Are you kidding me? I guess I have to fill you in."

Blake was really angry that he had to tell his dad, but his dad wasn't surprised, as he knew he was in possession of the rings that Brian said were stolen. Blake hung up and decided he would call Captain Baines in the morning to make sure Brian had turned himself in.

At ten the next morning, Blake called Captain Baines. "Hi, Captain. Did Mr. Anderson turn himself in yesterday?"

"Nope. If I don't hear from him today, I've got to call the insurance company and bring him in. What do you know?"

Blake was very disappointed. *How could this happen?* "He did what you said, Captain." Blake was careful not to tell him too much to avoid giving Baines any ammunition for later on. "Do you think you can go easy on him? I'll go get him now and give him a ride. But he's coming in on his own."

"I understand, Mr. Brennon. Bring him in, and we'll go from there. Let's see how he cooperates."

"I will see you in less than an hour." Blake hung up his landline and called Brian. No answer. Blake was really angry as he stormed out of his condo and headed back to Westminster.

Blake screeched up to his door, taking up three parking spots. Blake pounded on the door. No answer. The front door was unlocked, so Blake went in. On the couch was Brian. He wasn't breathing and looked pale. To the side of him was a note and an empty bottle of pills. Blake knew that Brian was dead.

Blake called 911 and then Captain Baines. The Orange County Fire Authority was there in minutes, and Baines was right behind them. An EMT pronounced him dead and looked to Captain Baines, who ordered his men to do a few crime scene evaluations, including some pictures. After about thirty minutes, everyone left except Blake, Baines, and the corpse. They were waiting for the coroner's van.

"What did the note say?" asked Blake.

"Here. You can read it."

Dear Hubert. My only real friend. I'm so sorry to end it like this, but I just can't face you and others after what I did. Don't blame Blake. He had to do what he did. My health has been bad, and I was faced with going to an assisted-living facility that I couldn't afford. Life is just too much for me. And, Hubert, I give you my Super Bowl rings, my only possession that is worth anything. I also leave you anything else I have. Brian Anderson

Blake tried to hold back the tears as Captain Baines took back the letter. "I'll have to hang on to this, but I'll fax you a copy to give to your dad. I suspect that's Hubert."

"Thanks, Captain. It's really weird to see Brian lying there. Where is the coroner?"

Just as he said that, two very fat men came up to the door. They identified themselves, got the okay from the captain to remove the body, and put his dad's friend on the gurney for a trip in the unmarked van.

"I'll take care of the funeral. Let me know when I can pick up the body," said Blake.

"Sure. Give me a couple of days after the autopsy. It's pretty clear, but we have to go by the book."

"Thanks, Captain. By the way, can you call the insurance company? Maybe just say he found the rings?"

"I'll do what I can, Mr. Brennon. Good luck."

Blake stood in the modest apartment and felt guilty. Was he too hard on his dad's friend? Did he drive him to this? What was he supposed to do now? Brian didn't have any family, so Blake guessed he had to take care of things. The first thing he had to do was call his dad.

24

Blake and his dad decided to split the cost of a small funeral. It seemed like just yesterday Blake was at Tiffany's funeral. The day of the funeral, Blake and his dad, Hubert, were astonished to see the number of people packed into the chapel at Forest Lawn in Cypress.

"I guess he had a lot of friends. Look at all the coaches and former football players that are here. He touched a lot of lives, Dad," said Blake.

"He sure did, son. It's too bad we didn't know this before. We could have all helped him."

"I don't know, Dad. He was so independent. I don't know if he would have welcomed handouts. Look, here come several Rhino players. There's Flash Gordon! Hi, Flash!"

"Hi. I forgot your name. I'm sorry. I know you used to date Tiffany," said Flash.

"I really didn't date her, but I'm working to find her

killer. I'm Blake Brennon from SRM. Do you know anything that could help me?"

"No, she was liked by everyone. She would help Doc a lot with all the doctor stuff. You know, get the medications from places and stuff. She was a big help to Doc."

"She got medicine for Doc?"

"Sure. She even picked up prescriptions and had them filled for the players. She was a big help. We all tipped her pretty good. She was cute, huh?"

"Yes, she was. But you mean she would go to all of your doctors and pick up prescriptions?"

"Mostly it was just from one doctor. He worked with Doc, so it was easier on us during the season."

"What doctor was that?"

"I gotta go sit down now. The minister is starting to speak."

"Whoa, Nelly," said Blake. "What doctor?"

"Doctor Tortolano. He's been helping Doc for a couple of years now."

"You don't mean Doctor Anthony Tortolano, do you?"

"I don't know his first name. But I rode with Tiffany over to his place a couple of times. I can't remember the name of it."

"The Green Briar?"

"Yeah, that's it. Nice place. Very quiet. But I really gotta go. I want to pay my respects to coach Anderson."

"Thanks, Flash. I'll be in touch. Hey, Dad, you want to hear a coincidence?"

"Sure, but you know what Grandpa always said about coincidences."

"Yes, I remember—that rock don't roll—and this one is too much to fall in the 1 percent of coincidences that are just that. This doctor Tortolano is in on almost everything I'm working on. He's got a basketball player imprisoned in his sanatorium, and now I find out he has ties to the Rhinos."

"Careful, Blake. You know how you can jump to conclusions, but I've got to say it sounds fishy to me. We've got to go sit down now. Crank up your brain later."

Blake and his dad sat down in the back. Blake listened intently to everyone who spoke. His dad had a tear running down his right eye. Blake was trying to forgive Brian for lying and deceiving him. Blake was still a bit angry but felt bad for his dad.

After the funeral, Blake accompanied his father in his car. They drove a few blocks to a reception at Perry's Pizza, Brian Anderson's favorite restaurant. More than one hundred people showed up, about half of the audience at Forrest Lawn. He told the owner, John Perry, there would probably be about twenty-five.

The next thing Blake saw was his father working behind the counter to help John. They had known each other for years, and Blake was Perry's friend too. Blake decided not to help because he wanted to corner Doc Strogham. "Hey, Doc. Can I talk to you a minute?"

"I don't know. Do I need my lawyer? The last time I talked to you, the police were grinding me the next day."

"Sorry about that. These murders are tough, and I never seem to finish a conversation with you. Do you know Anthony Tortolano?"

"Of course. He's kind of the quasi team doctor. But I'm the one the guys come to."

"What do you use him for?" asked Blake.

"I can't write prescriptions, so he has to do that. I tell him what I need. Sometimes he asks to examine the players. He saw Cadillac some before he died."

"Really? How does Tiffany fit into all of this?"

"Well, she was kind of my runner. She would help me pick up the Rxs and medications. As we already talked about, some of the medications went right to the players from Tortolano, if you know what I mean."

"I understand," Blake said, remembering their conversations about steroids. "Did she work for you or him?"

"She was a cheerleader. She just helped us both out. During football season, everyone is really busy."

"I understand, Doc. Does he refer the players to other doctors?"

"Not really too much. I send the player where he needs to go. I take care of them. Am I going to get in trouble because of the steroids?"

"Not from me, Doc. Not from me. Just keep playing

straight with me, and I'll help you all I can. If you lie, all bets are off."

"I got it," said Doc.

Blake ordered a pizza and Diet Pepsi from his father and sat down with the mourners. His dad charged him full price. He wondered how it would be to just attend functions or games without wearing his sportswriter's hat. That hat was on snug tonight. Blake's mind was racing a mile a minute.

25

Blake said goodbye to his dad and others and then went home to think. There was a message from Pet. Blake called her back. "Hi, Pet."

"Hi, Blake. Sorry about that bloke you buried today. How are you doing?"

"I'm all right. It's just that I could have been a little more understanding with him. I just thought he was conning me."

"Which he was. It's a good thing you are always straight-up with people. Right, Blake?"

"Yeah, I see what you mean. What's up?"

"I would like to come over and comfort you. What say you?"

"What say me?"

"Sorry. King's English comes out now and again."

"Well, anyway, not tonight, Pet. I really should see Blank tomorrow so we can update each other. Do you think that will be okay?"

"Just a minute." Blake could hear Pet talking in the background. "Yes, that's good, Blake. Come in after nine. Take care, love."

Blake said goodbye and wondered who she was talking to. Must have been Blank. She called from her cell and not the sheriff's office, so he couldn't be sure. All Blake knew was that whatever she did, he took to heart. Could Blake be in love with her?

On that note, Blake went to Bed. It wasn't Pet he was thinking about. All he could think of was Dr. Tortolano. Why did he seem to be at the crux of everything Blake was investigating?

The next morning, Blake awoke from a fitful sleep, got dressed, and drove to Blank's office. Pet met him with her cheerful smile.

"Hi, Blake. You missed me last night. Go right in."

Pet always had a way with words. She looked gorgeous today, but that would have to wait. He walked back to Blank's office.

"Hi, Blank. Let's fill each other in."

"Hi, Blake. Let's do that. We found out that Dr. Tortolano is affiliated with the Rhinos, but Doc Strogham seems to be our man. He was injecting steroids, so he injected the potassium. His son goes to first string, gets a big raise, and everyone's happy, except Cadillac, of course."

"I don't know about that, Blake. First, he swears he didn't kill Cadillac. Then, what about Tiffany?"

"Blake, the last ten killers I caught swore they didn't do it. He has the motive, the means—"

"I know, I know. But there is one other thing. The medical examiner told me that if you inject potassium, he would die right away. They use the stuff in executions."

"Well, then how did Cadillac get so much potassium in his system? How else can that happen?"

Blake thought about it but didn't have an answer. "Blank, let's hold off on arrests. There could be bigger fish to fry. And what about Tiffany?"

"Did it ever occur to you that Tiffany's murder had nothing to do with Cadillac's?"

"My gut tells me it did. And remember that note she had? Tortolano's name was on it. Maybe's he's involved."

"Okay, my gut will hold off while your gut finds stuff. My gut won't hold out much longer. By the way, there is a hearing about Rameesh today. Thought you would want to know. Why don't you take Pet to lunch and then go over to the courthouse? His agent wants to spring him from Green Briar."

"He should be sprung. I'll do that. Anything else?"

"That's it for now. Except I've been trying to get some of the Rhino players to tell me about any prescriptions given to them by Tortolano. They aren't talking. Maybe they will to you."

"I'll give it a try, Blank. Talk to you soon."

Blake walked out of Blank's office and made a beeline to Pet. "Blank says to take you to lunch. Can you go?"

"He already told me to go to lunch with you and pump you for more information. Let's go!" said Petula, affectionately known as Pet to Blake.

Blake always questioned her veracity. Sometimes she would omit some things, but she was honest, most of the time. Blake thought it was the cynical journalist coming out in him, but he couldn't seem to trust her 100 percent.

Blake drove her to the Bat Rack. Pet was wearing a black skirt and that see-through white top, this time with the lacy black bra. Frankly, it drove him wild.

Blake and Pet split a huge pastrami sandwich that came with two pickles and coleslaw. Pet spoke first. "Let's get bloody business out of the way first. Any secrets I can pass on to Blank?"

"None. How about him?"

"Nothing, except he really thinks Doc Strogham is Cadillac's killer. He's frustrated because you don't think so."

"He doesn't have any proof. He has him on giving steroids, but if they were legally prescribed, then even that's shaky. And then there's Tiff's murder ..."

"Yes, yes, I know all that. You just said all that to Blank."

"How did you know that? I just came back from talking to him. You haven't spoken to him, have you?"

"Blake, Blake, Blake. I tape everything that goes on in his office. In California, both parties have to consent to being taped, but we've used it to our advantage anyway. I'll tell you stories later. Anything else new?"

Blake thought this was definitely the only person he felt intimidated by. But Blake answered anyway, trying to look into Pet's gorgeous eyes. "You know everything already. Why the lunch?"

"Oh, Blake, I always get Blank to do what I want. I wanted to have lunch with you, so I used a pretense. Any problems?"

"No, I like having lunch with you too. But I do have to go to court now in that Rameesh thing. How about—"

"Fine. I'll see you at your home at seven, and I'll make you spaghetti and meatballs."

"How did you know I liked spag … never mind. I'll see you then. I'll bring some Chianti."

"You're on, good-looking. And I'll find something to wear that you'll like. Bye."

Pet walked out of the restaurant strutting like she had just conquered her prey. But Blake didn't mind being her prey or anything else. He could see her smiling, knowing he was looking at her. But now it was on to the courthouse to see what was happening with Rameesh.

Blake drove about three miles to the Santa Ana, Orange County Superior Court and found department 4, the room the hearing was set to be in. Blake saw Sam Klein, Rameesh Lewis's attorney, standing in front of the door to department 4.

Klein spoke first. "Hi, Mr. Brennon. Why are you here?"

"I'm just here because I'm sort of investigating what happened to Rameesh. I really never got to see him. The only thing I know is that Dr. Tortolano is very rude and will not give me the time of day."

"That's interesting. Please stay in the courthouse in case I need you. Okay?"

"I guess, but I don't know how I can help." Blake sat down in the audience as Klein sat down at the plaintiff's table, on the right side, facing the bench, and two lawyers and Dr. Tortolano sat on the left. Blake was surprised there weren't more people there. Sometimes the ex parte hearings were done quite suddenly, and people were unaware of what was going on. This was another situation where his association with the sheriff's office paid off.

26

The usual court pleasantries and introductions were accorded after the judge came in. Judge John Cannon was a pleasant man but only if no one tried to get one over on him. Then he became a tiger. Blake remembered a case where a wife of a baseball player tried to sweet-talk him into believing her story about spousal abuse, a precursor to their divorce.

He had her arrested for being under the influence in his courtroom of what turned out to be cocaine. The wife settled everything else quickly.

"Your Honor, I asked for this hearing to request that you immediately order the release of Rameesh Lewis from the Green Briar sanatorium so he can get the proper care he needs," said Sam Klein.

"Sorry to break in, Your Honor. That statement infers that Mr. Lewis is not getting good care at Green Briar. We resent the accusations," said a tall, skinny lawyer named Jack Fish, who was sitting right next to Dr. Tortolano.

"We have not been able to talk to Mr. Lewis, and I have his agent (another person working in Klein's office) and a reporter who have tried. We want an immediate release," argued Klein."

"Always glad to oblige," said Fish. "How about right now?"

The doors to the back of the courtroom dramatically flew open, and in walked Rameesh Lewis. He was not smiling and sure didn't look like the professional basketball player everyone saw playing a few months before. Rameesh sat down next to Dr. Tortolano.

Judge Cannon spoke next. "I don't like the drama, Mr. Fish, but are you saying you are releasing him right now and will not readmit him right away? I wouldn't like that."

"Dr. Tortolano decided to release him today after reviewing his case. Mr. Lewis has made significant progress and will go home after this hearing," said Fish.

"Your Honor," said Klein, "we assume we can talk to Mr. Lewis right after this hearing?"

"If he wants to talk to you," interrupted Fish again.

"Your Honor, we respectfully ask that you formally release Mr. Lewis so we don't all have to return tomorrow," said Klein.

"We have no problems with that, Your Honor. Mr. Lewis is really released. Right now!"

With that, Judge Cannon officially ordered the player's release from Green Briar. The court was adjourned. Blake could see Dr. Tortolano talking briefly to Rameesh, and the defense attorneys all left Rameesh sitting in his chair. Sam Klein and Blake made a beeline to him.

"Rameesh, are you okay?" asked Klein.

"Sure. I'm just tired. I wanna go home and sleep."

Blake had to get his questions answered. "Rameesh, were you held against your will? Why did you go there in the first place?"

After Klein told Rameesh who Blake was, the tall basketball forward unfolded out of his chair. "I was feeling depressed, so I went there. I don't know nothing else."

Blake thought that last part of his statement was odd since he wasn't asked anything else. Blake pulled Klein away from Rameesh and told him, "That rock don't roll. I want to talk to him again."

"I understand, Blake. I appreciate your help, but I have to do the best I can for my client. Please don't contact him. Call me in two days, and I'll decide what I can give you. I will give any info to you before any other media. Thank you."

Blake felt a bit rebuffed but understood Klein's position. It was interesting how Tortolano produced Rameesh just like that, and Rameesh looked like he was hungover and disturbed. There was a lot more to this, and Blake was going to find out what was up.

Anyway, it was time to head home and get ready for

Pet. He always had to prepare for her—what to tell her, what not to tell her, and to be ready for her omnipresence. But it was all worth it. Blake was mesmerized by this beautiful and unpredictable woman.

Pet arrived right on time, dragged Blake into his own bedroom, and said four words: "Take your clothes off." He did, she did, they did.

Afterward, they were lying in bed, and Blake said, "Wow. What was that all about?"

"We always talk shop before we make love. I wanted it different tonight. Any objections, love?"

"No, but I have meatballs burning on the stove." Blake was making her meatballs.

"I was going to make them for you, but go ahead and fix your meatballs, Blake. I'll be right out."

Blake put on his boxers and a robe and headed out to the kitchen. He turned the stove off and got out the pasta. He was hungry, especially after his surprise.

About ten minutes later, Pet came out of the bedroom fully dressed, just as she had entered his home before their lovemaking. She was wearing tight jeans and a plaid shirt tied at her tiny waist. She put her boots back on, giving her a whole new look.

"Well, cowboy. I sure enjoyed the ride. How are your balls doing?"

"They're all doing great. Dinner will be served in about five minutes. I'll pour us some wine."

"You mean me wine and you grape juice. Forget it. You don't have to get me drunk for another round. How about some diet soda?"

"Sounds great. Have a seat." Blake dished meatballs and thin spaghetti right from pans and plopped them down on the table. Pet had already put a two-liter bottle of soda on the table and got plastic cups from his cupboard.

"So, now we can talk shop," said Pet. "How come you were so wrong about Rameesh?"

"Boy, you sure get right to the point. I don't know. I just can't figure it out. I still think Dr. Doom did something to him."

"You mean Tortolano? And by the way, I didn't hear you complaining about being tired and in pain when I came in."

"Okay, okay. You never cease to amaze me. Anyway, I hope to see Rameesh and his lawyer in a couple of days to see what more I can find out. What does Blank think?"

"He thinks there is nothing there concerning Rameesh. He wants me to convince you that Doc Strogham is the murderer. All we got Tortolano for is distributing steroids, and really, it appears Tiffany did that."

Blake thought the only way Pet could know that update was if she had talked to Blank just before she came through the door. He had just left the courthouse two hours before.

"It does appear Tiffany was delivering drugs," said Blake. "But Doc didn't kill anyone. It's a gut feeling. Tortolano is my gut feeling for the murders."

"How is that, Blake? He's not going to kill a player who took steroids and then kill his runner. What good would that do him?"

"I don't know, Pet. But I'm going to find out. That rock really don't roll."

"Well, Blake, thanks for the dinner, but I have to rock and roll. See you tomorrow?"

"What? How about seconds?"

"That's all the pasta I can eat for one night. What time tomorrow?"

"Tomorrow, I'm taking off for some doctoring."

"What's wrong?" asked Pet.

"Oh, nothing really. I have a toothache, and I want to get my ears checked. I've had a little trouble hearing certain words at times, especially at ball games. Nothing serious. I just want to get me fixed."

"You're really too young for either of those problems, love, but you take care of yourself and call me when you're ready."

"That I will, Pet darling. You know I will. Bye."

Pet picked up her cowboy hat, which Blake hadn't even noticed when she came in. She threw him a kiss and blew out the door as fast as she came in. Blake would never be able to figure her out. How important was it to do that? Blake walked to the TV set to turn on Sports Center.

27

The next morning, Blake answered his landline. It was Liz. "Hi, Blake. Remember us? Rex wants to know if you are still writing for this magazine."

"Of course I am, Liz. Tell Rex I'm just about done with the Rameesh story. I'm taking off today for some medical appointments. The ENT doctor says my hearing aids are ready, and I need some dental work. Hey, do me a favor and make me an appointment with Dr. Tortolano, will you?"

"Sure, I'll call him right now. I assume you want it ASAP, right? You have to get that story in soon."

"Yes, tomorrow anytime would be great. Thanks, Liz!"

Blake just about got into the shower when his phone rang again. "Hi, Blake. It's Liz again. Dr. Tortolano said he wouldn't talk to you if you looked like Dolly Parton."

"Thanks, Liz. I'll drop by there tomorrow."

Blake finally got his shower in and dressed in casual

clothes to visit his doctors. The ENT went well, but Blake was sore after the dentist. He went home and watched sports on TV but fell asleep during an important hockey game.

The next morning, Blake woke up early, and his mouth was more swollen than ever. He called Dr. Kunihiro, the dentist he met earlier, and complained about the pain. "Docta Keneheo, ah need halp! Ah'll be right ova."

Blake put on the same clothes he wore the day before and headed over to the dentist office. The nurse brought him right in. Dr. Kunihiro followed in five minutes. "Hi, Blake. Whoa! Did you get in a fight?"

"No, damnit. You dit this ta me."

"It was a rhetorical question, Blake. Open your mouth, keep it open, and don't bite down. Then, answer my questions."

"How can I—"

"Oh, shut up, Blake. It looks like the filling was rising in the tooth. I'll smooth it out, and you should be okay soon. I'll give you some pain killers, but don't drive or play football."

"How do I—"

"You take the pills after you get home, Blake. Take them and call me tomorrow if you don't feel 80 percent better."

"Okeh. Tank you."

Blake got down to his car only to find his cell phone

ringing. "Hi, Blake. This is Liz. How did the interview with Dr. Tortolano go?"

"I cudant go taday. Half to go tamarow. Bad tooth."

"Okay, Blake. I'll put Rex off one more day. Good luck. By the way, can you hear me better?"

"What? Oh, my hearing aids. Yes, much better. Bye!"

Blake went home to watch Sports Center, but the pills he took knocked him out for the night. Blake woke up the next morning and felt much better. He decided it was time to pay Dr. Tortolano a visit.

This time, Blake put on a suit with his red power tie. He knew that was a little bit 1990s, but he felt more powerful in it. *Much like a businesswoman feels in a short skirt, open blouse, and very high heels*, he thought.

On the way to Green Briar in Garden Grove, Blake thought about how he would approach Doctor Doom, if he had a chance to talk to him. Blake walked through the double doors and straight to the receptionist. "Hello, I'm Blake Brennon, and I have an appointment with Dr. Tortolano. Is he in?"

"I'm sorry, Mr. Brennon, but I was the one who distinctly told your secretary he would not see you. He told me he doesn't like you."

"Tell him I am writing a story about him in *Sports Register Magazine*, and it would be better to have his side of the story in it."

"I'll see." The woman got up and walked back to Dr.

Tortolano's office. It was about fifteen minutes before she came out and said, "Come with me." She pointed to a big office down a long hall, and Blake walked back to the double doors and walked in. There sat the doctor, and behind Blake were two of the biggest goons he had ever seen. And Blake knew a lot of big people!

"Hello again, Doctor," said Blake.

"What part of *I don't want to talk to you* don't you understand?"

"I'm just trying to understand why—"

"Are those hearing aids you are hiding so conveniently behind your ears? I can't imagine a guy that's about forty needing hearing aids."

"Yes, well, I don't need them for everything, but all these years and all the screaming at sports events have apparently... yeow!" Blake felt a pain behind each ear and soon realized that one of the Bubbas had pulled off his hearing aids.

"You wouldn't have recording devices in there, would you, Blake?" asked Dr. Tortolano. "Bubba, as Blake calls you, you go check them out. Giant, you check Blake for any other recording devices."

Bubba left the room, and Giant walked toward Blake. Blake thought it would be better to hand Giant his recorder in his breast pocket, to save wear and tear on Blake's nice suit. He did and then said, "What in the world has gotten into you? I'm just here to ask some questions for a sports article I'm writing."

"You've been a pain in my butt for some time. I know that even if you were out of the picture, there are others right behind you, so you ask your questions, and let's be done with it."

"Okay. Why were you so secretive about Rameesh? Even his wife and lawyer couldn't get in this place."

"Rameesh didn't want to see his ex-wife, his lawyer, you, or anyone else. He was deeply depressed."

"You did a great job of curing him, Doctor. And now he doesn't want to talk about it. Strange, huh?"

"Not to me. They usually don't want to dredge up old hurts. You know what I mean, Blake?"

"Yes, I guess I do. Now what about the football team? You know—"

"What football team?"

"The one you are the doctor for. The Rhinos."

"Don't know anything about them. And you know what? If you continue to make those wild accusations, I will sue you. I don't get involved with sporting events, and you can't pin me down to any steroid use. Everything is off the books. You'll never get any proof of anything. Oh, here are your hearing aids and little recorder. You need new ones. These got broken somehow. But you're right, they were hearing aids. And here is your recorder."

Who said anything about steroids? Blake thought.

"May I suggest, Blake, that you leave me out of your

future investigations. Your mom and dad don't want to deal with me."

"Are you threatening me, Dr. Tortolano? And my family?"

"I don't know anything about your family in Culver City," lied the doctor. "But if you bug me, it's only fair that I bug them, right? Now I suggest you leave before Bubba and Giant throw you out. I will not talk to you again!"

Blake got up, carrying his ruined hearing aids in one hand and his recorder pieces in the other. Blake got in his car and drove out of the parking lot. Blake thought about his next move. And what did the good doctor mean about not getting involved in sporting events?

28

Blake picked up his cell phone and dialed Sam Klein, Rameesh's lawyer. "Hi, Mr. Klein. Can I see you and Rameesh ASAP? I need your take on this."

"I'm sorry, Blake, but Rameesh has no comment. In fact, he's sitting here in my office right now."

"Please, let me hear it from him, okay?"

"Sure. I owe you some for the help you gave us. Here he is."

"Um, hello. This is Rameesh."

"Listen, Rameesh. Dr. Tortolano told me everything, so if you can help me, we can put him away," bluffed Blake.

"He did? Hey, I didn't shave no points, no matter what he said," said Rameesh.

"Blake, this is Sam. He misunderstood what you said. That was off the record."

"It's on the record, Mr. Klein, or Sam. But I'll be as

discreet as I can in using it. Perhaps you can give me something off the record so I can find other sources."

"Off the record? Okay. He didn't shave points for Dr. Tortolano, so he was put in Tortolano's dungeon. If it hadn't been for you and me, I'm not sure he would ever have gotten out."

"But, Sam, why isn't he going to the police now?"

"You met his wife and kids. Tortolano threatened them. He can't say anything. If you repeat any of this, his kids could be killed. You might be in danger too."

"Thanks, Sam. You've helped a lot. I'll get back to you."

Blake hung up the phone. Things were starting to make sense. Tortolano was not just involved in the steroids but also possible big-time point-shaving. Now Tiffany's notes made since. "Tortolano, steroids, points." It wasn't just the steroids but also making sure teams didn't make their point spreads. It was time to visit Blank and write a steroids story.

Blake drove to the sheriff's office and walked in the front entrance, spying Pet as he walked in. "Hi, Pet. Aren't we dressing conservatively today?"

"Didn't know you were coming, Blake. Want me to take something off?"

"Yes, but I need to talk to Blank first. Right away."

"Go on in, love."

Blake walked back to Blank's office and found him in a meeting. Blank saw him and ended his meeting.

"Come on in, Blake. What's up?"

"The pieces of the puzzle are coming together. I think Dr. Tortolano was supplying steroids, and that gave him the leverage to make the players shave points. He used Kyle 'Doc' Strogham somehow—and maybe Tiffany a lot. But he's behind it all. Even murder would make sense if he felt threatened. And by the way, he just threatened me and my family and Rameesh and his family as well."

"Will Rameesh testify?"

"No, but I will."

"That's good, Blake. But we need proof. I'll talk to some of the players and Tortolano himself. But without proof, he'll walk."

"Then let's work on that. Let's get what we need to do that. By the way, don't mention Rameesh to Dr. Doom. That was off the record."

"I won't for now, but I may have to later. There is no off the record to the police. But I'm playing ball with you now, Blake. Now I'm going to call on Tortolano."

"Give me two days on that Tortolano interrogation, will you, Blank? I have to do some things first."

"You got it, Blake. So do I."

Blake talked strategy with Blank for more than a half hour before finally leaving his office. Pet was waiting for him when he went by her desk. "How's your mouth? Hello, can you hear me?"

"Very funny, Pet. I'm sorry I haven't called you. I have

to get my hearing aids repaired, and my mouth is almost ready to have you over if we don't get too rough."

"You know me, Blake. I can be as soft or as rough as you want. What's up? Why did you come in?"

"I just ran through some clues with Blank. He can tell you. I gotta go."

Blake went back to his house and nursed what was left of his sore gums. There was a message on his recorder that his hearing aids would be ready the day after tomorrow. He needed everything to be ready to face Dr. Tortolano once he found out Blake wasn't scared off and indeed even went to the police lieutenant with his allegations.

Blake got out his Mac and started to write his story. But he might have a lot more to say in a few days. He would put off the magazine and write a fluff piece about a basketball player who was found in bed with his mistress. It happened a few months ago, but Blake would write under the heading of what drives athletes to do whatever they want, whenever they want.

Blake got a lot of information in SRM's morgue, the print media room where past stories were indexed and kept. It was hard to keep his mind on that story. A big one was just around the corner.

29

Blake called his dad right after a lengthy call to his travel agent. "Hi, Dad. I have a surprise for you and Mom. You are going on an all-expense-paid cruise to Hawaii for two weeks. You leave tomorrow."

"What the hell are you talking about?" said Hubert Brennon.

"Listen, Dad, I have a guy that won't be inviting me to Thanksgiving dinner this year. He has threatened you and Mom, and he knows where you live. My travel agent, Laurie, has made all the arrangements. You leave from San Pedro Pier, not too far from your house. The shuttle will pick you up at one o'clock. Have a nice trip."

"Son, you be careful. This guy doesn't sound good. I'll go, and Mom will love to go. I won't tell her why. Anyway, she really likes the buffet."

"Yeah, Dad, and I know you do too. Take your cell, and I'll be in touch. Bye."

Blake was bracing for the worst, but he was in too deep to get out now. A couple of days passed, and Blake got in his "athletes above the law" story, got his hearing aids back, and waited to see what Tortolano's next move would be.

Blake's cell rang, and it was Liz. "Blake, nice story on the athletes. Rex said you forgot to add Michael Vick to your examples."

"Old news, tell him."

"We already added Vick. Say, I have a message for you."

"What is it?"

"Some guy says he wants to meet with you in the east parking lot at the Christ Cathedral at eleven o'clock tomorrow night. Says to come alone. He has information you need. What the heck is this about?"

"It may be the call I've been dreading but waiting for. Call him back and tell him I'll meet him."

"He said you'd be there. No return number. I told Rex about it, and he said not to go alone."

"Don't worry, Liz. I'll tell Lieutenant Blank Smith about it. I'll call you the next morning. Liz, I'm going to email a file of stuff I'm working on. If for some reason I don't come back, make sure someone follows up on the bastard."

"Blake, why are you talking like that? Should I be getting Rex involved in this? You know, this is just a sports magazine. We're not used to all this drama."

"Nope. Like I said, Liz, the police will be all over this. I'll see you in a couple of days."

The next day, Blake met Blank at the sheriff's headquarters. Blake only said hello to Pet and walked right into Blank's office. Pet followed him in and spoke first.

"What in the world is going on? Why are you here, Blake?"

"Sit down, Pet," said Blank. "You too, Blake. Blake is here to be outfitted for a wire so maybe we can get something on Tortolano. Right now, we don't have any proof to win a case against him. Blake is going to meet an informant tonight."

"And we'll be there too, right?" asked Pet.

"Right. We'll have men all over the place."

Blake broke in. "He said to come alone. I'm not sure we'll get anywhere if a bunch of cops are there."

"He'll never know until we swoop down on him tonight after eleven," said Blank. "There are plenty of places for us to hide at the cathedral. Blake is not going in there alone. If this is about Tortolano, he might have already killed two people that we know about. This is not TV. We're not sacrificing anyone."

Pet chimed in. "Let me go with you. He won't suspect a girlfriend."

Both men said no at the same time as a young-looking man came in to outfit Blake with the wire.

"My name's Gates. Now, sir, please take off your pants and shirt, and we'll get you wired up."

Pet said she would leave the room, but Blake asked why. Blank didn't blink. He obviously knew the two had been intimate. Blake stripped down, and Gates put the microphone on Blake's chest, with another one on his leg.

"This way, if one goes down, the other will still work. Press the button on your chest, and it activates the mics. We can activate it from here as well. We now have a fifty-mile radius, so there's no problem from anywhere in the county. This is the latest in technology and worth a lot of money, so be careful."

"Yeah, I will," said Blake. "I'll get this back in fine working order. Me too, I hope."

"It's not too late to back out of this," said Blank. "Maybe we can get some of the players to crack on him."

"They have a lot to lose. It will be easier to do that when he's behind bars. And besides, he threatened my family and others, as well as me. I want him. I'm a bit scared. It looks so easy on TV. And they solve it in an hour."

"Everything is easier on TV. I've got the warrant from a judge for this, so legally, we're all set."

Pet looked worried. "Love, how about I keep you company until tonight."

"Pet, I've got to think of what I want to say and what I want the pigeon to say. I also have to think of the way I want to protect myself. I need to be alone, but thanks."

"Okay," said Blank. "Get out of here, and remember

the password phrase, *that rock don't roll.* We'll be on you worse than Pet when she's horny."

Blake felt a little embarrassed, but he always felt Blank was in bed with him and Pet, figuratively of course. "Got it, Blank. See you tonight."

Pet walked Blake out, and he felt like dead man walking. Pet gave him a peck on his lips and hugged him. This was out of character for Pet, who was always very professional in the office. Blake walked out after giving Pet a fake smile and assured her he would call tomorrow even though he knew she would probably be part of the listening team tonight.

Blake drove to the Bat Rack, which was just across the street from Christ Cathedral, to eat and think. It was almost five. It was still six hours until his meeting at the cathedral. Blake walked in. There were plenty of tables that early, so he took one in the back. Blake wasn't sure his stomach could take anything, so he ordered an Arnold Palmer and salad. Blake was starting to regret this whole idea, but he had to do it. He just had to.

30

Blake was still sitting at his table at 9:00 p.m. when the loudspeaker went on in the Bat Rack. "Will the owner of a black BMW with the last two numbers on your California license plate zero seven please go to your car? It was damaged in the parking lot,"

Oh great, thought Blake. *That sounds like my car. That's all I need tonight.* Blake walked out to his car and saw a woman standing next to it, saying she was sorry.

Blake looked down at his vehicle and didn't see any damage. The next thing he knew, he had what felt like a gun in his ribs, with a man waving at him to get into the car parked next to his. Blake acquiesced.

Blake found himself in the middle of two big guys, one of them holding a gun firmly at his head. Of course, it was Bubba and Giant. Where were they taking him?

"I would like to know what is going on," Blake finally protested. But still nothing was said. Finally, the car stopped, and Blake was led across a parking lot. He was at the Green Briar. This was not good.

Blake was stripped down to his boxers and T-shirt, exposing the double wire put on just hours before. As he figured, it was Giant and Bubba doing all the work but not saying a word. He was then tied to a chair. Finally, Dr. Tortolano came in.

"Hello, Blake. Thank you for making your last trip to my office. Nice boxers."

Bubba finally said, "He's clean, boss. You want me to yank his hearing aids too?"

"No," said Tortolano. "I want him to hear what I have to say. We already checked them before. Blake, can you hear me?"

"I can hear you. What is this all about?"

"This is about you not heeding my last words to you. This is about you messing in my affairs. What did I tell you last time we met?"

"I heard you, Dr. Doom." Just then, Blake felt a crash and a pain on the left side of his head. Apparently, Bubba or Giant didn't like his choice of words.

"Now, Blake, please don't anger my boys anymore. They already hate working late, and they're missing hockey on TV. Now, why did you go to the cops about me?" asked Tortolano.

"I don't know what you're talking about."

Bam! There was another fist to the other side of his head from behind. Blake was in trouble.

"How about if we start telling the truth so my lie detectors don't go wild, huh, Blake?"

"Okay. Was it you I was supposed to meet at the Christ Cathedral tonight?"

"Well, I did set up a meeting, and a high school football player will be there to give someone information on a molestation by his coach. I hope all those cops you have there won't mind," said Tortolano.

"But why all of this for just steroids and maybe point-shaving?"

"Oh, Blake. You sure are naïve for an investigative reporter. If the word got out that I was asking players to, uh, alter the scores of the games, some of the bookies might not like that. They set up the spreads, we take the underdog, or an over-priced favorite, and the points and make sure the winning team doesn't cover. Capisce?"

"So you killed Tiffany because she was going to rat you out?"

"Sure. She was going to tell you, and that wouldn't make me look good. Right, Blake?"

"But what about Cadillac? What did he do?"

"Oh, poor Cadillac didn't cotton to my request on the points. I gave Doc some potassium chloride shots and pills, said they were steroids. He gave them to Cadillac all week before the big game. Just the right dosages. He died, and you know what? The Rhinos couldn't cover the spread. I made a lot of money."

"So the steroids were really just to suck the players into your debt so they would play ball, so to speak."

"Now you get it, Blake. But I did charge a lot for the steroids. Kept my hands out of it, thanks to runners like Tiffany. You could really write a great story now, right? As much as I like your stories, you know I can't let you live, right?"

"Just one more question. Was Doc involved in this at all?"

"His son knows all about the steroids and point-shaving. We just threatened to whack his dad, and he caved. But Doc was only involved in the steroids side. Funny, he was a real health nut, but he went for the steroids for the players."

"Why kill me, Dr. Tortolano? I just won't write the story. That rock just won't roll!"

"And how do I know that rock won't roll? If even a hint of this came out, I'd be a dead man. Those bookies would make me into chicken feed. They really don't like their spreads altered."

Just then, two police officers in full SWAT gear jumped through the window, spreading glass everywhere, with guns pointed at the three men. The other sheriff deputies came through the door. Tortolano, Bubba, and Giant were on the ground. Blake sat in the chair, still tied up in his underwear.

"Hi, Blank. Nice to see you. Did you get all that?" asked Blake.

"We sure did. Loud and clear," said Blank as he untied Blake.

"Wait a minute," protested Tortolano. "We didn't say a word until we pulled your mikes off. I just invited you here for tea."

"Sorry, Dr. Doom," said Blake. "When you ruined my hearing aids last week, I decided I really didn't need them, but I did get a great recording device that looks just like hearing aids. Aren't they neat?"

"But how did you find us?" asked Tortolano, looking up at Blank from the floor. "We even set up a decoy car in case you were following Blake. And of course, you were expecting us at the cathedral! On top of that, we left Blake's cell phone at the Bat Rack. A lot of them have GPS in them."

Blank answered, "Oh, didn't Blake tell you? He has a GPS device in his tooth. Just had it installed. We knew the Christ Cathedral meeting might be a ruse or even just a starting point. But Blake had the 'hearing aids' and the GPS on since five tonight. Or is it last night by now?"

"Blake," said Tortolano, turning his head to the right, "if you publish this story, I'm a goner, even if I got off legally. You know that."

"Yes. It might behoove you to cop a plea and keep this quiet. Of course I will write my story. Probably a three-parter. But tell your buddies, Dr. Doom, that all sports reporters are going after steroid suppliers, and users, and point shavers. Murder and threats just don't intimidate us anymore. Of course, you probably won't have any buddies anymore. They have a tendency to get amnesia about arrested friends."

Dr. Tortolano was dragged out along with Bubba and Giant.

Blank turned to Blake. "Great work, Blake. Come on down tomorrow morning so I can get an official statement."

"I will, Blank. I will. Can you give me a lift back to the Bat Rack?"

"I'll get your car home, Blake. There's an officer downstairs who will take you home. By the way, put on your clothes, will you?"

Blake put on his clothes and walked downstairs to meet the officer who was going to take him home.

"Hi, love," said Pet.

"Hi, Pet. You are a sight for sore eyes! Please take me home."

"I will, Blake. Why don't you get in the back and lie down? I'll drive."

Blake did that and fell fast asleep.

31

Blake woke up in his bed the next morning at eleven with Pet looking at him. "Hi, sleepyhead. Come on downstairs for some vittles."

"Uh, okay, Pet. Give me a few minutes, will you?"

"Of course. I'll see you then. By the way, I called your parents on the cruise and told them you are okay and they are safe. And to have a nice time. I told them you would call them later. I also called Liz and told her you would call later. Okay?"

"Great. By the way, how did I get in my bed?"

"I called Blank. He knows that firemen stuff. You were really out like a light."

"Oh great. Blank was in my bed! Anyway, I'll be right down."

Blake showered, got dressed, and joined Pet at the kitchen table. Pet had some questions. Pet looked sexy in just a T-shirt and jeans. Her ponytail highlighted her sexy, high cheekbones and face.

"Blake, what would you have done if Dr. Tortolano confiscated your earpieces?"

"I didn't think he would, because he had already done that before. And especially after he found my police mics on my chest and legs, he thought he was safe. And besides, I had the tooth GPS."

"Do you think he would have killed you?"

"No doubt about it. He had already killed twice. I think he would have killed me and gone underground to avoid the bookies."

"And how did you get the idea to use a GPS in your tooth?"

"Actually, it started with the Rocket Wallace kidnapping. In my investigation, I found that GPS devices are now very small and can be placed just about anywhere in the body. I went to Dr. Kunihiro, the same dentist I know, and he put it in for me. Then it was just hooking up to you guys and hoping you'd bust in Tortolano's office in time."

"What if he killed you right away, maybe even at the Bat Rack?"

"Tortolano was very egotistic. He wanted to rub my nose in it and even impress his goons."

"Are you sad Tiffany was in so deep?"

"I think she was going to tell me the night she was killed. I feel responsible in a way."

"Blake, she chose her way of life. We are all responsible

for our actions. You aren't to blame. Now, what is this point-shaving thing the bloke was involved in?"

"Let's say you call your bookie and want to bet on the Lakers over the Knicks. The bookies post an educated guess that the Lakers should win by ten points. The spread is ten points. If you are a player on the Lakers and you are winning by nine points with time running out, if you missed the last shot, the Lakers would have won the game but not by the spread of ten points. That means the Laker betters would lose! Same goes for that *slip* before making another touchdown."

"So the players can still win their game but make money if the score is closer than anticipated?" said Pet.

"Yes. These days, the players make so much money that sometimes methods other than money are used, such as blackmail, threats, and even murder.

"By the way, Pet, tell me the truth. What is with you and Blank? I always seem to think his interests come first, certainly before mine."

"Now, Blake, how can you think I've been anything but honest with you? Blank and I work well together. That's it. He asked me to get information from you. I told you that, and you gave it to me. You used me too. After that, it was just you and me."

"By the way," continued Pet, "Blank called and said Giant and Bubba are singing up a storm to avoid the gas. Tortolano's lawyer is meeting with the good doctor now on how to save his life from the bookies. We got them."

"Well, that's great, Pet. I've got to start on my story for *Sports Register Magazine.* I'll need some pictures. Can you get some of the sheriff's pictures?"

"Of course. Anything you want. By the way, Liz said she thinks you have another Pulitzer in hand. She needs it as fast as possible to beat the newspapers. Don't worry. Our lips are closed to them for a few days. I'll come back tonight to make you dinner. And dessert."

"Thanks, Pet. That would be great."

Blake waived goodbye to Pet. He still didn't understand where he stood with her and wanted to find out. He could fall in love with her, if only he knew if she could fall in love with him. For right now, he had successfully investigated the biggest story of his life. For right now, that rock did roll!

BOOK II

32

"Well," said Blake's secretary, Liz, "you managed to go through all of that in one piece."

Blake answered, "I thought I would write on sports and avoid the pitfalls of regular news investigative reporting. I think I'll ask Rex if I can cover badminton."

Rex Harrington was Blake's boss at the *Sports Register Magazine*, a weekly sports magazine that understood they couldn't do sports stories that people could read a week before on the internet or in a newspaper.

Blake Brennon wrote human interest and feature articles for the *Register*. Rex kept him on his toes by asking what he had done for the *Register* lately.

"I don't think that Rex has you in mind to write about badminton. He wants to see you right away," said Liz.

SRM's western office was in Santa Ana, California, about ten miles north of Blake's home in Newport Beach. Really, the whole country was Blake's beat, but there was usually enough going on with the sports teams in Orange County and everything in Los Angeles County. Orange County Stadium was used for both baseball and football until the new stadium would be built for baseball.

"Come on in, Blake," said Rex. "I know you have nothing to do, so ..."

"Hey, I was almost killed, and I'm up for a Pulitzer on the murder story. I thought I would ask for a couple of weeks off," stammered Blake.

"Maybe after this assignment. We have to keep the readers happy. And now we are online too. Gotta keep the stories coming in. We just got a tip that the Titans football players are being poached by another college and luring their football commitments away from them."

"That happens all the time, Rex. It's legal if they follow the rules."

"I know that, Blake, but the players appear to be offered money, houses, cars, and more. That is not legal. At least not now. Go see what's going on."

Blake left Rex's office knowing it was impossible to change Rex's mind. *Maybe that's why he's such a good manager.* Blake looked over the sparse notes Rex had given him and decided to visit the coach of the local university. It was just prior to the football season, and he was in his office.

"Tex Buenafe?" asked Blake. "I'm from the *Register*

magazine. I heard about you losing commits, and it doesn't look good from where I sit."

"I know who you are, Mr. Brennon. I wish you guys could write more about our team. I know we should play in NCAA Division II, but we are trying to win here in Division I. Yes, we have been told another team in another state is offering inducements to our commits. We couldn't do that here if we wanted to. We don't have the money. But these are good players, and we could have been great this year. We offered wonderful scholarships and room and board, but we understand they are getting money and much more to play in addition to the aforementioned."

"This is a big story, Tex. Is there any reason on your end why I shouldn't pursue this?"

"I know we are clean. Like I said, I don't know how I would personally fare if I was a whistleblower. There's probably a lot of teams that would prefer this didn't come out because they might be doing it too."

"That certainly could be the case, Tex. But this issue has to come to a head. Teams have to compete fairly and within the rules. But with the schools making millions and the bookies making more, there could be real problems in the future."

"But remember, Mr. Brennon, the millions the universities make on football pays for all the other sports too. I know it sounds weird, but I make a lot more than the rocket scientist professors. I put the product on the field that makes the millions. I won't be here long if I don't win."

"That's right. But we have to strive for a level playing field. I'll see what I can find out. I'll get back to you," said Blake.

Blake got the name of the other university and left the three-hundred-plus-pound head coach of the Fullerton State University Titans. This looked like it might be a bigger mess than he thought.

On the way back from the university, Blake stopped by Perry's Pizza in Garden Grove to enjoy their hot ham and cheese sandwich and buy a lotto ticket. Blake bought at least one every week, using the same set of numbers comprised of uniform numbers of his favorite baseball players. He never came close to winning, but it was fun. Blake fantasized about what he would do with millions of dollars, but that lasted as far as his sandwich did.

Back at the *Register* office, Blake called Colossal College in Iowa to ask them about the recruits.

"Mr. Bright, I'm Blake Brennon from the *Register*. I heard a rumor that you have been recruiting players already committed to other football teams. Is that true?"

Jeff Bright was the football coach at Colossal.

"Mr. Brandon," said Bright, "I have been talking to committed recruits. There's nothing wrong with that. We have a great school here—a nice campus and we offer a great education. It's very appealing to the kids and their parents."

"But the rumor has it you are offering bribes to the kids. If that's true, that rock don't roll. By the way, my name is Brennon."

"Rumor might have me making eight million a year, but my wife would be very surprised if that were true. When you have proof, go to the NCAA."

The NCAA was the governing body of more than a thousand colleges split into forty conferences. They oversaw twenty-four sports, men's and women's. The National Collegiate Athletic Association was under fire to pay students, and that was winding its way through the courts.

"But unauthorized bribing will never be," said Blake.

"Never happens here. Go to the bigger universities. They even give their players' parents cushy positions with the teams," said Bright.

"So your position is you do everything right, Mr. Bright?"

"And yours is that you act on rumor, Mr. Branklin. Goodbye." Bright hung up.

Blake did tell Bright he was acting on a rumor, so as not to implicate the Titan coach. He couldn't blame him, but he thought that Bright was very defensive. But Blake could put Bright in the *rock that don't roll* mode.

33

Blake woke up Sunday morning and started to read his newspaper. When he got to the lotto results, he looked at five games going on in the state and the country. When he got to the California lotto, he had to go back to the numbers again. He was used to just glancing at them, but these numbers he would recognize.

7 Mickey Mantle's number with the Yankees. Famous old-time player.

24 Walt Alston managed the Dodgers for more than twenty years. Blake's dad liked a quieter approach.

29 Dale Long played for the Hollywood Stars minor league team just before the Dodgers came to LA. Later, he went to the Stars' parent team, the Pittsburgh Pirates. He was still tied for nine games in a row for hitting home runs for the Pirates. Blake's dad's favorite player.

53 Don Drysdale was a great pitcher for the Dodgers in the 1950s and 1960s. Blake's dad's favorite pitcher. Blake was beginning to see a theme here, influenced by his dad.

The mega number couldn't possibly be fourteen. That was Mike Scioscia's number when he caught for the Dodgers in the 1980s. *A nice guy and a very reliable player. My dad got to meet him one time and became his fan even though Scioscia went on to manage the Angels for nineteen years.*

Yikes! It was fourteen.

Blake pinched himself to make sure he wasn't dreaming. After hours of looking at the numbers and trying to breathe, he finally thought of what to do next.

His first rational thought was to make sure it wasn't a misprint. He saw the same numbers four times on TV. The same numbers were in the paper the next day.

He called his attorney, Dwight Spenser, a longtime friend and Rotarian buddy. Spenser said he would check into it. Meantime, the ticket needed to be copied, put in a good place, and no one but Spenser came in or out of his home. Spenser assured Blake he would have everything in place by the next day.

Blake assured himself he wouldn't do anything differently in his life, as he liked his job and was happy. He did think he might be even more desirable to women, however. But he was going to try to keep this a secret. He had heard about all the problems people had.

Blake decided to stay in his home that Monday. He didn't answer calls, and there were many, and he couldn't concentrate on the TV—even the scores of games. He couldn't sleep. He couldn't eat. His head was spinning. He knew he should wait to count chickens. Nothing he thought of seemed to make sense. He would not tell anyone else until he made sure that rock would roll.

The next day, Blake went to his office.

"Hi, Blake," said Liz. "Did you have a nice day off yesterday? Here are your messages. By the way, Rex wants to see you, as always."

Blake turned right and went into Rex's office. "Hello, Rex."

"You know, Blake, you have been a great reporter for a lot of years here. But if you aren't coming in, I expect a call so at least we know what to tell people when you are coming in. I tried to call you several times," said Rex.

"I work six or seven days a week. I can take a day off anytime I want."

"Almost true, but I need to know where you are. Liz was worried about you. It hasn't been that long since you almost bought the farm. And besides, I'm your boss, and I'm entitled."

There were a few things running through Blake's mind. But Blake said goodbye and told Rex he was taking the day off after he checked his messages. Rex was puzzled, as he had never experienced this before from Blake. But he didn't say anything more.

Blake checked his messages and thought he could call them back the next day. Nothing seemed to be that important. Actually, *nothing* seemed important anymore. Blake left and went to the city of Orange to see Spenser.

"Congratulations, Blake," said Spenser. "I triple-checked the numbers. Let me see your ticket."

Blake handed Spenser the lottery ticket. Spenser checked the numbers and date.

"You are a multi-multi-multimillionaire, Blake. How does that feel?"

"I'll believe it when I see a balance in my checking account. What do we do next?"

"Here is a list I compiled for you. After we talk, we are going to the lottery office on Baker Street in Costa Mesa. That is, after you talk to your CPA.

"First," said Spenser, "don't tell anyone you won the lotto. I can give you stories you won't believe, and I will later. Second, don't do anything for sixty days. Don't quit your job, don't buy expensive cars or boats, and so on. Wait and think hard about it. Third, talk to a good CPA and discuss taxes, both now and the future. Fourth, talk to a good financial advisor. Discuss maximizing things with a very good retirement-planning lawyer. Me! Prepare an estate plan with an experienced estate-planning lawyer. Me! I can do that. Consider charitable gifts to help people. And last, get out of debt and don't get into debt in the future. Any questions?"

Blake and Spenser talked for about an hour, but there were still many questions in Blake's muddled mind.

Blake decided he was in no condition to meet with the lottery people and make lifelong decisions. "I will wait and hear from a couple of people first," said Blake to Spenser.

Blake said goodbye to Spenser and said he would call him in a couple of days and set up a time to go to the lottery office. Blake put the ticket in his safe deposit box and decided he wouldn't tell anyone it was there. If anyone got a hold of it, it was their ticket! Spenser warned Blake about delays but he wanted to make some decisions first.

34

Blake's cell phone rang. It was Liz. "Got a call from one of your spies about a murder of a cheerleader at a local high school."

"Didn't we have a story like that in Texas years ago?" asked Blake.

"Yes, we did. But this is now. And besides, maybe the mother of another cheerleader didn't do it this time."

"Well, I don't have time right now."

"Rex said you do have time."

"Tell Rex to ..." Blake stopped in his tracks. He didn't want to quit or give any clues to his fortune. "Tell Rex not to worry. Text over any information you have."

Blake lamented this was just what he didn't need. He had two possible hot stories and didn't want to spend any time on either of them. But he didn't want to let down his boss or his magazine. At least not right now. And besides, he really wanted the magazine to prosper in a time when a lot of print media was being replaced by amateur social media.

Blake called Orange Grove High. He talked to the principal and was told the sheriff didn't want him to talk to the media. That meant he had to call the sheriff's lieutenant, Blank Smith. He was named Blank because he was the last of ten kids and his mother just left it blank on the birth certificate and never changed it. Blank thought it was unique and never changed it himself.

"Hey, Blake. Thought you'd never call. You are calling about the cheerleader death, yes?"

"Yes, Blank. Can you tell me anything? My boss is all over me."

"Not much to tell. I can't give you the name, but a sixteen-year-old girl was found dead behind the gym. She just made the cheer squad."

"Have you conducted any interviews, any suspects?"

"We should have some by now. It's been two days. Right, Blake? Anyway, you know I can't give you anything yet. I might consider throwing you a morsel down the line."

"I understand, Blank."

"You do? Are you sick? What am I going to do with my comebacks?"

"Please call me if anything cracks."

"Sure, I'll make notes on my desk to call you. Yeah right!"

Blake hung up and called Blank's secretary, who was a sheriff officer. Blake called her back rather than being transferred because he wasn't anxious for Blank to know he was talking to her. Blake and Petula saw each other at times, and each used the other as needed. It was a strange relationship, but Pet was beautiful.

"Hi, Blake," said Pet. "It's been a bloody long time since I heard from you. What do you want to pump me about today?"

"Hi," answered Blake. "I'll settle to just do the pump part."

"We'll see about that. But I get dinner before I tell you anything about the cheerleader murder."

"Was it a murder? I'm in the dark. And why do you think I want information?"

"You got something out of me already. What time tonight are you picking me up? And I'm sure you won't ask me about the murder."

"Pick you up at seven, Pet."

Blake just had time to visit his CPA, Willard O'Brian. The first thing O'Brian said was "Don't tell anyone! Okay, no one except your attorney and maybe a financial advisor. I can't stress that enough. I've heard about inheritances or people who came into a lot less money and were hounded by everyone. Okay, you have a list of questions? First let me say a few things.

"First, you won three hundred million dollars. You

have two choices. Pay the estimated federal tax liability of about one hundred and eleven million and then settle up at tax time for the rest, if any. Good news! California is one of the few states that don't tax lotto winnings. You save about thirty million there.

"Or you can get thirty annual checks. For this amount, about thirty checks for ten million each. You would then pay taxes as you receive the income.

"You have to figure out if you can do better than the annuity company who takes on the liability. It's a gamble. If the economy goes south, a lot of your money might vanish if you control it yourself instead of getting an annual check. If it stays relatively good over the thirty years, as has mostly been the case, you could come out ahead.

"Second, banks have limitations on what they insure. You could put money in all the banks, as the limitations are per bank. Municipal tax-free bonds are the usual vehicle for a lot of money.

"Third, stay in California. Thirty million dollars is a lot of money.

"Wow," said Blake. "That is a lot to take in. I suppose there will be interest made if I take the lump sum."

"You could make about 3 percent annual interest on your money. I really wouldn't worry about it. By the way, if you have any charities to donate to, that would be a good choice. Let me check them out to make sure they qualify for a deduction and are legitimate."

"Yes, my charity will be the Rotary Club. I will be in touch. Thanks, Will."

Blake left the CPA's Newport Beach office. His head was spinning. Now it was on to see Pet. Could he really keep this to himself?

Blake drove to Pet's home in Newport Beach. She answered the door in a see-through blouse. She was braless and a beautiful blond to begin with. He was forgetting about the $300 million.

"Come on in, Blake. How about a drink? Oh yes, you don't drink."

"I've had quite a day. Give me a Diet Coke."

"I wanted to loosen you up!"

"Believe me, I'm loose as a goose!"

Pet got Blake his Diet Coke, made a Long Island iced tea for herself, and sat down beside Blake on the sofa. "Tell me all about your day!"

"You wouldn't believe it if I told you. I can't right now, but maybe someday I will. So how is that murder of the young cheerleader going?"

"Not much to go on." Pet hesitated. "She was found strangled behind the gym. She had just made the varsity cheerleaders squad. She was still in her outfit, and it was just after practice. No weapon at the scene and apparently no clues."

"Looks like a dead end," said Blake. "In Texas, a few years ago, the mother of a daughter who didn't make the squad killed a cheerleader so her daughter could make the team. Anyone talked to the mother of the replacement?"

"They are interviewing now. Do you really think someone would kill to get her daughter on the cheer squad?"

"It did happen. And there have been cases of bodily injury caused for the same reason. Gotta keep an open mind."

"Right now," said Pet, "my mind is on something else. Another Coke?"

Blake and Pet retired to her bedroom. It was almost as beautiful as she was. There was little talking done the rest of the night.

35

Blake left her house the next morning after a great night. He was wearing the same clothes, but he made a luncheon meeting at the Garden Park Rotary Club. Blake's dad had been a Rotarian for almost forty years in Culver City, and Blake had for fifteen, there in Garden Grove. It was a club assembly, and the Rotarians were talking about finances.

Rotary clubs contributed internationally and had done wonderful things, like almost eradicating polio from then world, vastly increasing access to water, and much more. But they also did a lot for the communities they resided in. Garden Park was a small club, twenty-five members. Money was always a problem. They wanted to do so much. Blake really wanted to blurt out that money wouldn't be a problem in the future, but he had to think about it. Raising money for Rotary was a wonderful, but difficult experience. Would a large donation take that feeling away from some of them? Nothing was going to be easy.

After the meeting, it was time to visit the Costa Mesa Lottery office. Blake picked up Spenser, and they went down the 57 freeway, first stopping at the bank to get the lottery ticket, named lotto in California's game, and then walked into the lottery office. It didn't have a lot of people in it, so they just went up to the designated first responder.

"Hello," said Blake. "I won the lottery. Who do I see?"

"I hope so," said a young lady with a large tattoo on her arm. "I will get someone to help you."

Fifteen minutes passed before an older man who looked like a stereotyped CPA, including thick glasses, came out.

"Come with me, Mr.?"

"Brennon. Blake Brennon. This is my lawyer, Dwight Spenser."

He led them into a big office, and there sat five other people—three women and two men. One woman was a court reporter who started to take down the conversation. Blake and Spenser sat down as instructed.

"My name is Donald Smathers. Let me have the ticket." The ticket was passed around to all concerned, and they all checked the numbers against numbers on a sheet they already had. Smathers gave a receipt for the ticket to Blake, as well as names and cell numbers of all the people present except the court reporter. He took two pictures of Blake with the ticket and promised the one he was keeping would be kept confidential.

Spenser looked everything over and took notes. He had already made a copy of the ticket and had the copy notarized by two notaries.

Smathers continued, "It appears you have won three hundred million, four hundred and fifty thousand dollars. Congratulations, Mr. Brennon."

"Is this where I say please give me my check?" asked Blake.

"It's not quite that easy. First, we will notify the state lottery office, which will verify. Then we investigate your claim, which includes seeing if anyone else makes the same claim. Then a press conference to show what has happened, and then your check. It takes about a month. Have you decided how you want to take your money?"

"All at once and no press conference."

"As you wish. But you will be asked about this several more times. We like to advertise the winners to promote our lottery. By the way, have you been told that Uncle Sam will take a big bite if you choose to take it all?"

"Yes, and I understand, but I want it now. Personal reasons."

"I understand. We are all under strict secrecy orders here, but it doesn't always work."

Spenser interjected, "But that's the way we want it. I have all of your names, but I want the court reporter's name and the woman at the front desk."

"You can see the problem, Mr. Brennon. The media offers money for information, but we will prosecute any proven leaks."

Blake filled out a form, and his signature was notarized. He and Spenser left the building, and Blake thought everyone was looking at him.

"We did everything we could," said Spenser. "The penalty for leakers is small, so brace yourself."

Blake drove Spenser back to his office and proceeded to go to his SRM office.

Liz said, "Rex wants to know how your stories are coming."

"Tell him I am not going to cover the recruiting story. I will write a story on how the college athletes will be paid performers soon. I will follow up on the murder story. I got some clues last night."

"I agree with you, Blake. The college players story isn't big news. I will tell him, but you might get a call."

"By the way, there was a call that someone is buying Kobe Bryant's house in Newport Beach. His wife, Vanessa, said she didn't know if she could ever sell it."

"I know. The house isn't far from someone I know at the sheriff's office. It was tragic that Kobe died in that helicopter crash along with his thirteen-year-old daughter. Someone might want to look into it but not me."

"Okay, Blake. If there is anything I can do, please let me know."

36

Blake had a lot to ponder, but he didn't want to let down his employer. Blake went to Orange Grove High School to talk to the principal, George Haskel.

"I know this is a tragedy Mr. Haskel," said Blake. I know you don't want to talk to me, but is there anything you can tell me? I will help the police find the murderer."

"Lt. Smith called back and said I could talk to you. He said not to give you her name, but she was sixteen and strangled behind the gym in her newly issued cheer outfit. She just won the tryouts and just made the team. We were devastated. I was called, and I called the sheriff's department, who sent a team out right away. I haven't been told about any evidence. They investigated and took the body away. They said they would call her parents. The funeral is Saturday at St. Martin's."

"Thank you, Mr. Haskel. You gave me a lot of information. Any idea who it could have been?"

"She was very popular, as most, if not all, cheerleaders are. Maybe the cheer advisor, Miss Hong, can help you. She's just outside."

Blake thanked Mr. Haskel who went outside and sent Miss Hong in.

"I hope I'm not late. I had to get the new cheerleaders ready for our first performance Saturday night," said Hong.

"What's the new girl's name?" asked Blake.

"Vicki Nguyen."

"Is she new to the team?"

"Yes, we just had the tryouts, and she just missed making the squad. She was sure happy she finally made it, but I'm sure she was very sad to hear what happened to Rebecca."

"I'm sure," responded Blake. "Do you know why anybody wanted to kill her?"

"She just made the team. But Rebecca seemed very popular with the other girls and the judges. She had a great personality and was very flexible, and apparently a good dancer."

"A lot better than the next girl down, Vicki?"

"I liked Rebecca a little better. I voted for her. But you have to be at least pretty good to even be considered."

"It must be pretty tragic to barely miss something like this. I can only relate it to when I didn't make the football team when I was at Culver City High School."

"Girls are pretty emotional at this age. I think Vicki is sixteen. A few years ago, in Texas, a mother of one who just missed killed a cheerleader in much the same circumstances. Are you going to grill Vicki's mother?"

"Wouldn't that be weird if that happened again?" said Blake. "I don't know if she would talk to me. Perhaps you might not want to tell her about me."

"You don't think Vicki had anything to do with this, do you? She seems like a nice girl."

"In my experience, murderers don't all have gangster faces and personalities. You never know. But we'll find out. You can bet on that." Blake now knew the victim's first name.

Two days later, Blake attended the funeral at St. Martin's for the deceased girl. Her name was plastered all over the church and printed program. It was Rebecca Sterling. Blake looked around and sat behind some people who had been identified by Miss Hong as the Nguyen family.

"I can't believe she was killed," said Vicki. "Are we all safe?" She hung onto her mother for comfort.

An older person, who Blake guessed was her mom, sat on the other side of Vicki and told her it was okay. The mom said she knew that Vicki would eventually be on the team no matter what.

The boyfriend, a big football type, told Vicki he was happy to have a happy girlfriend—maybe not that day but overall. He was very consoling.

Blake listened to them talking and met mom Nguyen after the service. "Hello, ma'am. I am Blake Brennon from the *Sports Register Magazine.* I just wanted to get your take on the recent tragedy."

"My name is Silvia Nguyen. I have no comment. Please don't blame anyone in my family. We had nothing to do with it."

"But Vicki did make the squad. And Vicki, or people close to her, did have a motive."

"Do you think we would kill Rebecca to make a cheerleading team?"

"I did hear Vicki was very emotional about missing out. Almost hysterical."

Silvia Nguyen looked incredulously at Blake and asked, "Do you have teenage girls?"

"No, I don't. No kids. Not married."

"Then you have no idea. Girls get emotional about getting a C on a test. This was a big deal. But She got over it within two days."

"She got over it right after Rebecca was murdered?"

"That doesn't mean she would ever harm Rebecca. I will only talk to the sheriff from now on. This is ridiculous."

"I'm not accusing anybody, Mrs. Nguyen. The sheriff and I have to find out who did this terrible thing."

"I hope you do. Then come back and apologize to me."

"I hope to do just that, Mrs. Nguyen. By the way, is there a Mr. Nguyen?"

"Yes. He's never home. Goodbye."

Blake went to the Sterling home, where there was a wake in progress. Vicki's family was there.

On his way out, a teenage boy who Blake recognized came up to the family. Silvia Nguyen started the conversation.

"Johnny, Vicki isn't here yet."

"I've been trying to call her, but she hasn't returned my calls."

"She's been pretty busy with her new position on the cheer squad. By the way, Mr. Brennon, this is Vicki's boyfriend, Johnny Mai. Johnny, this is Mr. Brennon. He's a sportswriter for a sports magazine."

"Hello, Mr. Brennon," said Johnny Mai. "Mrs. Nguyen, when do you expect Vicki?"

"I don't know, Johnny. I'll tell her you came by."

Johnny turned around and walked back to his car. Blake walked out the door to his car. Johnny screeched out of his parking place and drove down the street.

Blake sighed as he remembered his days as a teenager and his fast wheels. He hoped his parents never found that out about him.

37

Blake didn't have a feeling about who could have murdered Rebecca. Vicki's mother seemed a bit cold, but could she have killed her daughter's rival cheerleader? Could it have been a random killing? It didn't look like that at all. It was time for another date with Pet to determine if the sheriff's office had anything more. And of course, Blake wanted more of Pet.

But before that, it was time to see about his lottery winnings. It wouldn't be long until he got his check. He had to tell his parents, but he wanted to wait until he actually got his money. His parents lived a comfortable life, but Blake thought at least $250,000 a year would make them more comfortable. They could travel and do everything they wanted to do and see. He couldn't wait to tell them.

Blake's attorney, Dwight Spenser, called Blake on his cell phone. "Hi, Blake. Can you come by my office and chat? I have some information for you. Or I can send a car for you, and you can pay for it."

"Thanks, Dwight. But I can drive. And I'm not too far away. Just south on Harbor and east on Chapman. I'll be right there."

He entered Spenser's office and went right in. His secretary said Blake could and that Spenser said he would be renaming his office as Blake Brennon's office. Blake knew she was kidding, but it was hitting him that having money was giving him great percs.

"Sit down, Blake. I have some news. You really didn't win any money."

Blake was feeling a heart attack coming on.

"Just kidding, Blake. A little Rotary Club humor!"

Spenser waited until the color came back in Blake's face. "I was notified today you will be getting a check for three hundred million, four hundred and fifty thousand dollars, less one hundred and eleven million, one hundred and twenty-six thousand dollars in federal tax withholding. California doesn't want your money. I suggest we go to the lottery office and pick it up. They require a receipt anyway. Then I found a consortium of banks that can give you insurance on most of the money. You can transfer any amount to your own bank as you wish, remembering the limits on insurance at that bank. You have a living trust that we will alter so you have up to one million dollars' insurance at each bank. Your check will be one hundred eighty-nine million, three hundred and twenty-four thousand dollars.

"We will go to your bank, or another one if you choose, and get them on board with what they have to know."

"When can we pick up the check?"

"Monday at ten. Okay? I will have a bank consortium representative meet us there."

"Sounds great. And if you ever do that joke on me again, I'll shoot you. By the way, will one million cover your fee for all this?"

"Yes," said Spenser. "I'll let you know when you owe me more. Any questions until Monday?"

"Yes. I want to give the Rotary one million dollars to start. As you know, we all take pride in raising money and doing wonderful things in the community and world. Yet we all complain about asking for money and spending our own. Will this change any of that?"

"As you know, we, the Rotary club, are a 501c tax-exempt charitable corporation. We have a board. We can make all the members advisors and can spend our time on banking and spending the money. I don't think it would be a problem, but I'll check it out without mentioning your name."

"Thanks, Dwight. Please take care of everything, and I will see you Monday in Costa Mesa at the lottery office."

"Great. See you then. And we should alter your living trust next week as well. As usual, mum's the word!"

"I hope so!" said Blake. "Boy, this rock sure ain't rolling smoothly."

"This is nothing. But I'm here to help, as well as others," said Spenser.

38

Blake called Pet and set up a date for Friday. Then he decided to visit his office.

"Hi, Blake," said Liz. "We haven't heard much from you lately. Here are your messages. Rex wants to see you."

"Thanks, Liz," said Blake as he strolled into Rex's office.

"Hi, Blake. Everything okay? I need some copy for next week's issue."

"I meant to talk to you about that, Rex. There is no story about the recruiting thing. It won't be long until college athletes will be paid. The richer schools will all have to form their own leagues with smaller schools, or ones that can't spend the money, will form B, C, and D leagues to compete."

"That sounds like a good story right there. Write it and have it on my desk by Monday," said Rex.

"Okay, but I will have it to you Tuesday. I need a couple of days off."

"Blake, I don't know what you are up to, but that's really the date I need it by. Do you need photos?"

"I think we have a shot of the Titans' football coach as well as one of the university, so I think we are all set," said Blake.

"Okay. I can get pictures of the NCAA logo too. This will be a great story," said Rex. "Now, what about the murder at the local high school?"

"I've done a lot of interviews, but I don't have anything. I have an important interview with the sheriff's office Friday."

Rex said, "Do you think the replacement girl's mother did it? You know, like the one in Texas a few years ago? That would really be a story wouldn't it?"

"No, I don't think so. In fact, everyone I have interviewed seems innocent. I haven't interviewed the mother of the slain cheerleader yet. I will talk to the principal and anyone else that might know something. I might even go to the game Saturday night at Orange Grove High School."

"Good idea, Blake. So much for your days off. Take Sunday off," said Rex.

"And when do you think I should write the college story?"

"On Monday?" answered Rex.

"Yeah, like it only takes a day to write a story like that. I have to call the NCAA and much more." Blake would have to tell him about his lottery winnings at some point.

"Then take a day off next week. You can do it!" said Rex.

Blake left his office building and drove home. How much could his mind comprehend? *College story, murder stories, and oh yes, this lottery thing.*

Blake spent the rest of that day and most of Friday contemplating what he was going to do with his money. He also called the NCAA to get their take on paying athletes and where that was going. Then it was time to get spruced up for his date with Pet.

Blake was attracted to Pet in a big way. She was gorgeous, sure, but they also seemed to click. But was Pet playing him? There was no doubt it started that way. Did she really like him now? Meanwhile, the sex was great, so he decided to see how it played out. And maybe he could get some information from Lt. Blank's right-hand deputy. Did that mean Blake was playing her?

Blake called Pet and told her to wear her little black dress.

"Not much notice, but I can do that. Where are we going?" asked Pet.

"It's a surprise, Pet. Be hungry."

Blake finished getting dressed in a nice suit and cuff links. *Pet won't believe it.* He went to pick her up at her nice home. *Maybe she inherited her house too! Is her daddy still alive?* Blake rang her doorbell. She answered and looked great in her little black dress. Low and short, top to bottom.

"Are you ready, Pet?" asked Blake.

"Sure. Do you want to come in for a drink?"

"No thanks. We are going to a nice restaurant in Newport Beach. We have a reservation."

Pet sashayed into his BMW. Blake didn't open the door every time for her, but he did this time. A short while later, they arrived at the Ritz. The restaurant was as ritzy as the name.

"Did you rob a bank, Blake?" said Pet.

"No, I just wanted to take you to a nice place."

The two of them walked in. A sophisticated woman showed them to a table. Menus came later. Blake was surprised to see prices on the menu. He was told fancy menus didn't have prices on them. Later, someone told him just the ladies' menu didn't used to have prices on them, but times had changed. The two of them looked them over.

"Blake, I can't order anything here. It's too bloody expensive!"

"As usual, it's on me, Pet. I came into a little money, so it's okay."

"I will pay half, okay?"

"No, that's fine, Pet. I really want to do this for you."

"You understand I will stay all night with you even if we go to McDonald's, right?"

"Either way, we can enjoy each other."

They ordered prime rib with baked potatoes, green beans with bacon, and a French dip of some kind. Blake ordered an Arnold Palmer, and Pet wanted champagne. The French onion soup was on its way.

"Okay, Blake. How much is a little money? I don't want Blank to check into your bank accounts. What gives?"

"Maybe I'll tell you later, Pet. But let's just enjoy each other's company."

"Okay, Blake."

The two had a romantic evening all through the dinner. Pet ordered two glasses of champagne. It was the first real conversation they ever had.

"While we are sipping our drinks," started Pet, "what have you found out about the cheerleader murder?"

"I've talked to just about everyone, and no one seems to be the one. I'm really at a dead end. What about your office?"

"We are the same way. Blank was hoping you would have something. Are you going to continue trying?"

"Yes, I'm going to the football game tomorrow night to nose around. Do you want to go?"

"No, I don't like American football. You Americans call football soccer. What is that blarney all about?"

"Actually, you call soccer football," said Blake.

"The rest of the world calls it football. It is the most popular game and name in the world. But whatever. Tell me what you find out."

"Okay. Let's go to my house. I have more champagne, I think."

Blake drove her to his home. She seemed sincere about her answers. Pet and Blake walked into his townhome. Neither was talking business anymore.

"Blake, that was delicious. I want to know what gives," said Pet.

"I really shouldn't talk about it. Have another glass of champagne from my home."

"Thank you. I will. But before you rip my clothes off, I want some answers."

"Let's just say I came into some money. That's it."

Blake then ripped her clothes off, as well as his. They didn't even make it to his bedroom. They never got out of the living room with the warm fire, low music, and very comfortable couch.

The next morning, they had an encore before Pet finally spoke. "Blake, you are going to tell me eventually. Why not clue me in?"

"Okay, Pet. You wore me down. Literally. I won the lottery. But no one can know, not even Blank or anyone else. I won't tell you how much, but it means we can dine out at a fancy place once in a while."

"Wow, that's wonderful, Blake. If you need any help, let me know!"

"You mean on how to spend it?"

"Please, Blake. Do I look like I bloody need to find someone with money? I've turned down billionaires before."

"I'm sorry," said Blake. "I'm just new at this. But I'm depending on you to keep this quiet."

"Of course I will. So what's next on the murder case?"

"The football game tonight, as I said before. I'm going to have to start really digging on this one, and so must the sheriff's office."

"I agree, Blake. Let's meet again soon. Remember, if there is anything I can do, I'm here."

"Thank you, Pet. Now, where were we?"

39

Blake got to the game early at Grove Stadium on the campus of Orange Grove High School, not far from Blake's office and north about twelve miles from his home. He perused the bleachers on the Orange Grove side and saw Silvia Nguyen, Vicki's mother, sitting next to a man. Blake sat next to her.

"Hello, my name is Blake Brennon."

"Yes, I remember you. This is my husband, Robert Nguyen. Are you and the police still hounding me?" asked Silvia.

"Not at all, ma'am. I just wanted to see a game. I haven't seen a high school game in quite a while. Where is Vicki?"

"She's there with the other girls in front of the field. And don't believe for a second I think you happened by," said Sylvia.

"Do you want something?" asked Robert Nguyen.

"Well, since we have some time, what do you have to say about this mess? I'm sorry your daughter and wife and you are dragged into it."

"I don't mind answering questions, Mr. Brennon," said Robert Nguyen. "It just seems like we have been grilled like suspects. I almost wish Vicki wasn't next in line for the cheer job."

"I understand, Mr. Nguyen. The sooner we solve this thing, the sooner your family is off the hook. Do you have any idea who could have done this?"

"Not in the least. It was a blow to the whole family when Vicki didn't make the original cut. Then the cheer advisor said Vicki was next in line if they needed a replacement during the season. But Vicki was devastated. She cried for two days."

"You would do anything to see her happy, wouldn't you, Mr. Nguyen?"

Robert Nguyen didn't answer for a few seconds, then did.

"She kinda perked up after seeing her boyfriend, Johnny. She really looked better just prior to, uh, finding out about Rebecca. And no, no one I even know could have done such a thing, especially over something as trivial as this," lamented Robert.

"I played football in high school," said Blake. "Making the team meant everything. And the Orange Grove cheer advisor said making the cheer team was the same thing."

"Yes." Robert sighed. "But with what you now know, you may have been a little too worried about all that, right? It's important to my little girl, but in the scope of things, it would have blown over, and we would all be back to normal. Don't you think?"

Just then, Blake saw Vicki madly talking to Johnny, standing on her side of the field fence, while Johnny was on the fans' side. "They seem to be having a spat," said Blake.

"Sure," said Robert Nguyen. "Stick around until after the game, and you'll see me trying to stop them from kissing."

"I don't know; they both seem mad. But she left him in a hurry. The kickoff is about to start."

"Good. Maybe things will get back to normal and we can see football and my little girl can do what she loves," said Robert.

Blake liked his answers. Blake would be defensive too with all the questions and hidden accusations from different sources. Blake liked to watch high school football. It was good entertainment and a great game to watch. The players were even better than the players when Blake played twenty-eight years ago. The plays were more sophisticated, and the coaching much better.

But Blake was watching cheerleader Vicki with one eye, the parents with an ear, and Johnny with another eye. Maybe Johnny knew if his girlfriend or parents were in on the murder. If Vicki and Johnny were to split up, he might be willing to rat on them.

Orange Grove beat Corona Lutheran 48–14. Vicki and the others had a lot to cheer about. The Nguyens looked proud of their daughter. It was time to look in another direction but not forget this one.

Blake said goodbye to the Nguyens and waved goodbye to Vicki, who was trying to get past Johnny and back to the dressing room. Both had words for each other again. *Young love*, thought Blake.

Blake left the field with nothing to hang his hat on. It was hard to think of Pet, the lottery, and investigative reporting all at once. But he was trying.

Blake left the field and went home. He had a story to write about the college players getting paid, he had a big appointment at the lottery office on Monday, and he had to fit Pet in there somewhere.

40

Blake sat at his computer on Sunday to write his story about paying athletes at the college level. As usual, he thought about the questions he wanted answered. He outlined what he wanted to say. He would fill in later with reasons and why and when.

> *Should college athletes be paid?* No, otherwise it's just a pro minor league. But the athletes should get much more than tuition, books, and room and board. They now have limitations on jobs and income by the NCAA and often go hungry for food and dates. Tell stories about athlete's problems. Give examples. Get quotes from NCAA, California legislators, coaches, and college presidents. And high school coaches.

If athletes are going to be paid, should all of them be paid the same? Yes, otherwise pro rules will become the norm, with athletes going to the highest bidder, and they will renegotiate as their skill level improves. A small number of schools might be left out in this kind of situation, while others cannot compete. College is great proving ground for athletes. The current rule is footballers can leave after their junior year. Basketball players can play one year and go pro. Explain relative value of all football positions. Wouldn't it change high school athletics, as the coaches would be hard-pressed to play everyone to showcase their talents?

Eventually, wouldn't high school players have to be paid? Using the pay-for-play logic, why not Pop Warner?

Less than 2 percent of college athletes make it to the pros, and a lot are cut before they play a down.

Wouldn't all college sports have to be the same? Sure, but only moneymaking sports can financially exist. That means that athletes in the other sports, aside from basketball and football, will have to pay to play.

What about girls' sports? Someday, at least basketball and soccer might be moneymaking sports, but this will set girls' sports back a long way. Right now, men's basketball and football pay for all college sports. Explain where I think this is going. Get women coaches' views.

Why this problem? College football head coaches make millions of dollars a year. Even some assistant coaches make millions today. Football, especially, makes a lot of money, from tickets, paraphernalia, TV, radio, and other things. But the student athletes don't share in this. Is this right? Give examples on both sides. Give my compromise ideas. Make it so all football and basketball players don't have to work to make money all year. Other sports, make it so they don't have to work in season. Boys and girls. Explain how athletes have to train and study their sports all year around. (Is it fair a rocket scientist professor gets a pittance [salary] compared to coaches?) Some of coaches' salaries paid by outside groups and persons. Quotes.

Explain laws in some states and the NCAA reluctance to face this issue. What will they do?

What happened to the Olympics after pros were allowed to play? Other countries were doing it before. Examples.

Compare to show some college athletes are getting paid, even if illegal.

Is it time to have noncollege amateur teams set up to play college sports teams? A lot of student athletes shouldn't take up space in classrooms. Although it is a myth, you can be stupid to play in big-time sports, if you are talented enough.

Suggest pictures to Rex.

Blake thought that should about cover it. Aside from some quotes he already had, he would get more tomorrow after the trip to the lottery office. Rex was right; this would be a good story, although it already had a lot of press. But no doubt amateur sports would change forever—not for the good, unless a lot of thought went into it and it was done right.

Blake got most if it done and went to bed early,

around ten o'clock. He ate a bologna sandwich first and lamented he wasn't eating much these days.

The next morning, he finished the story and drove it to SRM. Rex wasn't there yet, so he dropped it off and drove to his attorney's office.

41

He met Dwight Spenser, his attorney, at Spenser's office, and they drove to the lottery office in Costa Mesa, a city northwest of Newport Beach. They were to meet Mark Harmon, the assigned executive of the bank conglomerate that the money was going to be put in initially. He didn't look like a bank guy. He was ruggedly handsome, like he should be on the cover of Brawny paper towels. He brought with him a big security guy—at least six foot six and three hundred pounds. Not fat, all muscle.

And who was also there? Petula from the sheriff's office.

"Hi, Blake. I thought you might need some help."

"How did you find about this, Pet?"

"Come on. You said you won the lottery. You were busy Sunday and Monday. The lottery office is closed Sunday, and you mentioned you were going to see your lawyer Monday. I am a detective, you know."

"A detective? I thought you were a sworn secretary."

"I guess you don't know everything about me, Blake. I'll have to fill you in later."

"Okay, I guess you are here. Remember mum's the word."

"My mum will appreciate that," said Pet.

"Let's get started," said the lottery director, Donald Smathers. He introduced three other men and a woman, who all looked like the money was coming from their wallets.

"You will notice that we have a court reporter, Dixie, who will take everything down. You will get a copy of the transcript, Mr. Spenser. Okay, on the record. Let the record show that the following people are present and include the winner, Blake Brennon, and his attorney, Dwight Spenser, as well as a representative from the Orange County sheriff's office, Petula Clark." He then read everyone else's name as they all filled out attendance sheets on their way in.

"Mr. Brennon, you have entered and won the California Lottery. The amount is three hundred million, four hundred and fifty thousand dollars. One hundred eighty-nine million, three hundred and twenty-four thousand dollars is here for you. The balance will be sent to the IRS. Here is your check for one hundred eighty-nine million, three hundred and twenty-four thousand dollars, payable to you. Here is the check witnessed by everyone in the room, who will attest to this transaction."

Smathers gave the check to Blake. Blake again asked for complete secrecy, but he was getting nervous, as the number of people involved was growing.

"Your people may use the room to your left to discuss things. Congratulations to you. We are off the record."

Blake's entourage retired to the room on the left. It was a conference room with plenty of seats and a large table as well as telephones.

"Well," said Blake. "I don't know where to start. What do I do now, Dwight?"

His attorney and longtime friend said, "First, give me the check after you sign it. Mr. Levitt here from the bank conglomerate will take it and explain what will happen next."

"My name is Mark Levitt. I represent the conglomerate that will in effect be the custodian of your money. Your money, as long as it is kept in this conglomerate, is FDIC insured and spread over many banks. To you, it will be one account through the Bank of America. They have authorized me to give you these blank checks, and you can immediately draw on your account.

"Next, we have a minibus waiting outside to take your party and us to Los Angeles to deposit the check. Thanks to your sheriff's representative, Petula Clark, it will be followed by two sheriff's cars in contact with our van."

"We will also have a helicopter flying overhead," said Pet.

"Uh, thank you, Pet. Good idea," an overwhelmed Blake said.

"It's okay, love. You're paying for it."

"Anyway," continued Levitt, "Mr. Spenser has all of your deposit details and I'm sure will advise you, especially in the near future. Our van will bring you back here to pick up your cars."

Spenser, Pet, Levitt, the big security guard, and Blake climbed into the van. Blake saw the sheriff's cars in the background, and the helicopter was already overhead.

Was this really happening? It was a thirty-five-mile ride to the Bank of America corporate office in Los Angeles. People were talking to him, but he was in a fog. Later, he would remember telling Spenser to repeat everything the next day.

Finally, the van pulled up to the Bank of America offices. It didn't look like a bank, more like an office building. Inside, it had a feel of a large, plush office, with a lot of private offices. Blake was applauded as he came in. This didn't look good for his secrecy issue.

A very personable man, Henry Quan, led everyone into the conference room. "Are there any questions? We have deposited your check and given Mr. Spenser a receipt and a copy to Mr. Brennon. We have checks already printed for Mr. Brennon with a new account number—all different from any accounts you have now. As far as you are concerned, Mr. Brennon, you have just this one checking account for your lottery winnings. It is up to you to determine if you want to keep your old accounts with the balances you now have, and of course you can add to them or any other account from this new account.

"I have asked your local BOA branch manager to contact you to determine what other deposits you may want to make from your lottery account. I understand you have a financial advisor, but I can recommend one too if you wish."

"I think I have it all down," said a flustered Blake. "I don't want anything else now. I have to figure out what I want to do."

Then Dwight Spenser broke in. "I asked the lottery for complete secrecy, Mr. Quan."

"I didn't get that information. Usually it is the depositor who makes the request. I will ask everyone here to honor your request."

Blake knew it was an impossible task to keep this quiet. He would have to adjust that part of his plans. "Thank you, Mr. Quan."

"By the way," added Mr. Quan, "your lottery account will be handled from this office. It does take special handling, as you can imagine. By the way, you have some special ID designations I have given to Mr. Spenser. Be careful with them. You have almost two hundred million dollars here, and you never know what can happen."

"I understand. Thank you for your help."

Bank of America transported Blake and his attorney, Dwight Spenser, back to the lottery office to pick up their cars. Spenser told Blake not to do anything rash. He would see him in a few days and discuss things. Blake wrote him the first check out of his new account: $1,000,000!

"Thank you, Blake. I am always at your disposal. I gave you my private number. I am available twenty-four seven."

Blake's mind could not keep up with everything. His next revelation would be to his parents and brothers. He also had the cheerleader murder, and what would he tell SRM? And he didn't want Pet to think he disappeared, although she knew about this, and he really needed to talk to her.

42

The next day, Blake visited his *Sports Register Magazine* office.

"Hi, Liz. Sorry I haven't been in lately. Is Rex in?"

"Yes, and he wants to see you," said Liz.

Blake walked to Rex's office, expecting to be chastened. Instead, Rex asked him to sit down. "Blake, as you know, the print media is slowing down in this country, and we were slow to get our emagazine started. SRM is going to sell to a big conglomerate who will probably merge us with their sports magazine. It will be the end of SRM."

"What? I've been here forever," said Blake. "Do you think this magazine is a loser?"

"No, I think with some changes and a bigger emphasis on our emagazine, we would do well. But they think differently in New York, as you know."

"Have you told them about what you think?"

"I have, but they won't listen. They are stuck in their ways, so they want to be bailed out."

"Is this for sure yet?" asked Blake.

"No, they are meeting again at the end of this week. In the meantime, please continue what you are doing until we get the ax."

"Thanks, Rex. Let me think this over," said Blake.

Blake rushed out of the office, planning to go to his parents' house in Culver City, in the heart of Los Angeles County. Instead, he barged into his attorney's office. Dwight was with a client.

"Dwight, I need you right away."

"I'm sorry, Blake, but Mr. Corbin here stands to lose a hundred thousand dollars if we don't act soon on his case. Can you wait an hour or two?"

"No, I can't," answered Blake. "I will guarantee his hundred thousand dollars if he can come back tomorrow."

"You're on," said Mr. Corbin. "Get that in writing, Mr. Spenser."

"Don't need to," replied Dwight. "I'm a witness. Come back tomorrow afternoon."

Mr. Corbin left, and Blake sat down in front of Dwight.

"Dwight, I need some fast work. I want to buy the *Sports Register Magazine*."

"What?" stammered Dwight. "Why?"

"Not important right now," said Blake. "It's almost

sold as we talk. I need you to find out some details about circulation and so on. And it has to be fast. The final meeting is set in New York on Friday. Here are some telephone numbers and names. Can you do it?"

"I will do it," said Spenser only half-convincingly. "Let's meet Wednesday. I will get several people on this, including telling the brass at the *Register* to hold off the sale and you might buy it."

"Don't tell them I'm in it. Not yet."

"Okay, as you wish. Now get out of here, and I'll see you Wednesday."

Blake left and called his parents on his cell phone to make sure they were there. They were. Blake was on his way up the 405 Freeway to Culver City, the city of many movie and TV studios and where Blake grew up. He went to Culver City schools and played football, baseball, and basketball at those schools. Blake thought he would remember to send money for the sports and arts programs in Culver City schools.

It took about an hour, but Blake finally made it to their house, a nice little three-bedroom home that was very neat and clean, on Dobson Way where Blake grew up.

"Hi, Mom and Dad. I need to talk to you."

"Sure, son. You're going to live, aren't you? Please don't pussyfoot around with something serious," said his dad.

Blake's parents were wonderful parents to Blake and

his brothers, Jim and Joe. His dad had become a little impatient now that he was sixty-eight, but he was in great shape and still a great father. His mom offered big love. She had enough to go around. Although subservient to her husband, they had been married for forty-six years. It was a good marriage, and they took good care of each other.

His mom always put up pictures of whoever was visiting, so she didn't like surprise visits. But she was always glad to see her children. Blake was the oldest, followed by Jim in two years and Joe four years after that.

Blake sat on the thirty-year-old sofa, and his mom and dad sat down on the chairs directly across from him in the small living room. "Mom, Dad, I won the lottery. Here is a check for one million dollars. More later, and I will buy you a house. And I paid the taxes. It's free and clear. If I give away more than twelve million total, I will pay federal estate taxes after I die. But the recipients never pay any tax."

Blake's parents both looked at him. Blake wasn't sure they understood him. They had blank looks on their faces and couldn't speak for a couple of minutes that seemed like an hour. Then his dad stood, his mom stood, and they both walked over and hugged Blake. "Congratulations, Blake," said his dad. His mom was crying. "It couldn't happen to a nicer boy. I don't know what I will do with the money, but we could use a few things around here."

"Let me make you lunch," said his mom. "I'll make you your favorite. Potato pancakes and homemade tomato soup with noodles. Thank you, Blake."

His mom went to the kitchen, and Blake and his dad talked.

"I haven't talked to Mom yet, but I think we'll stay here. Buy some new furniture, paint the house, and so on. I wouldn't mind a new car with the newfangled toys on it. Mom needs a new car too."

"Anything you want, Dad. But I will buy you a new house if you want one. This one is fifty years old!"

"Yeah, but there are a lot of memories here. See here where we marked every year how tall you and your brothers were all getting? Mom does need some more room for more pictures, however."

"You and Mom decide and let me know if you ever run out of the one million. Now let's eat!"

Blake had a lunch consisting of potato pancakes and tomato soup with special noodles. Blake promised himself he would be back for more in the near future. And after that too!

His mom gave Blake a big hug, and even his dad did. Now it was about time to see his brothers. He called them and asked them to meet at his house that evening. They asked why. Blake wouldn't tell them, but they agreed to come. He did tell them it would be worth their while. Mom and Dad promised not to spill the beans to them.

Jim and Joe Brennon arrived at six. Jim brought some sandwiches and soda for them.

"Okay, Blake, what gives? Why the mystery?"

"Yeah," said Joe. "Hand over those sandwiches."

Blake finally spoke up. "I asked you both here without your wives and kids because I have something for you. I want to leave it up to you to tell them in your own time and way. First, let me say you two are the best brothers I could ever have hoped for. Except when Jim cheated on me in a Ping-Pong game when I was twelve and he was ten. And then there was—"

Jim said, "Come on, Blake. What gives? There's a football game on in thirty minutes."

"Okay. I have a check here for one million dollars for each of you. Tax-free."

"What bank did you rob, Blake? Geesh, or is this a joke?" asked Jim.

"It's no joke. And I want to do something for the wife and kids. I need you to tell me what's okay. Money sometimes turn people into weirdos. No hurry on that. Maybe in a month or so."

"You have got to be kidding, Blake. This will change our whole lives! How much did you win?"

"I'd rather not say for now. When your family asks, just say I came into a little money."

"Yeah, and he gave us a little bit. One million," said Joe sarcastically.

"Be careful what you say to anyone, and they must be sworn to secrecy. And the less people that even know my name, the better. Capisce?"

"Blake, I don't know what to say. This is mind-boggling. How can you even handle this?" asked Jim.

"I have a lot of help. But I have been warned that if people find out, I will be hounded for money."

"Thanks, Blake," said Joe. "I'm not really hungry. Thanks anyway for the sandwiches. I will take the check though."

"You both are welcome. I gave Mom and Dad a check too. I haven't even spent anything outside of that though. I know you want to get home. Let's meet in about a month, all of us and the families, and celebrate, okay?"

"You bet," said Jim and Joe in unison. "Our treat!" Both figuratively kissed Blake's feet and left in a stupor.

Blake decided to call Spenser and ask him how he was doing. "Any luck on buying the *Sports Register Magazine*?"

"I did get them to hold off on the sale. But it will take about seventy-five million dollars. Are you prepared to spend that?"

"I am," said Blake. "But see what you can do to get that down. Is it worth that much?"

"The other party offered seventy million. I haven't had time to go over the tangible assets versus the potential yet. They are faxing information over now. As an investment, I'm not sure you'll ever get that back."

"I understand, Dwight. But I have a lot of myself invested in SRM. Do what you can, but I'll go that high without another phone call."

"Okay, Blake. You're coming in tomorrow, so I'll go over everything with you then. Make it at noon, and we'll go to lunch."

Blake concurred, hung up, and went to bed. He was just about asleep when Pet called.

"Blake, remember me? How about dinner later? And Blank wants to see you tomorrow. Can you make it?"

"Yes to the dinner and no to Blank. I can see him Thursday morning."

"Jolly good. Why don't we meet at the Bat Rack. We haven't been there in a while."

"Sounds good. See you at eight."

Blake went to sleep. Luckily, he set the alarm for seven, because it woke him up after three hours of sleep. It was off to the Bat Rack.

43

Driving up to the Bat Rack reminded Blake of when he was kidnapped and could have been killed. Although it ended good, he knew it must have taken years off his life. But meeting Pet made him feel younger. If only he could shake that feeling that there was something more to her than he thought. But as soon as he saw her, that thought jetted from his mind.

"Hi, Jet. I mean Pet."

"Hi, yourself, whatever your name is. You know you are buying dinner," said Pet.

"I always buy dinner."

"I know, but I was going to buy tonight but changed my mind."

"That fine. What does Blank want to see me about Thursday?"

"Boy, right to it, huh, Blake? He wants to know if winning the lottery affects your helping on the cheerleader case."

"No one knows it. Does he?"

"I had to tell him. But don't worry. Everyone I tell your story to I make them promise not to tell anyone. And besides, he would think you robbed the national vault. He had to know."

"Okay. Only about a hundred people know now. I never want it advertised, but I think the cat is out of the bag."

"What cat, Blake? Anyway, I'll keep it quiet if you buy dinner."

"Good. Order anything you want. We'll quietly celebrate. Lobster?"

Blake had never ordered something off a menu and not look at the price. What fun! It was really exhilarating. Blake and Pet had a great meal and a Diet Coke and wine.

"Okay, Blake. Time to go to my home. I have Diet Coke and a beautiful nightgown. Are you up for it?"

"Yes, very up for it."

Blake paid the check with a new credit card that had no limit. *This is a different world*, he thought. He followed Pet from the Bat Rack to her beautiful home. He still couldn't figure out how she could afford it. Another mystery about Pet. The two walked into her home, where the lights were just right. Pet poured them drinks, and they had a few minutes for small talk.

Pet excused herself and came back in a beautiful negligee. Blake couldn't control himself. She had to be the most beautiful woman in the world. Not knowing everything about her became a nonissue. She was all woman, said the right things, and melted into his arms. They never made it to her bedroom. But her big sofa was just fine. Blake didn't think life could get any better. But could it get worse?

Blake didn't sleep all night. How could he with Pet lying next to him? No man could. He didn't have to leave yet, as he didn't have to be to his attorney's until noon. Pet told him to follow her up to her bedroom. He did. They did.

Blake reluctantly left at 11:30 a.m., wanting more. As he drove to Spenser's office, he wondered why Pet didn't go to work yet. *There I go again*, he thought. *Who cares?*

Blake drove to Spenser's office. He went right in like he owned the place. "Sorry about that, Dwight. I'm really in deep thought these days."

"I can imagine, Blake. Okay, let me give you the rundown. The other party wouldn't match the seventy-five million. It's yours if you want it. The *Sports Register Magazine* has three offices. New York, Chicago, and here in Southern California. Eighty employees. Very little debt that will be paid off by the sellers through escrow.

"The offices are leased. They have five and a half million paper subscribers, and I'm trying to get a real handle on the digital subscribers. Right now, they are sending over the details of everything. They want a five-million-dollar deposit that will be nonrefundable if the deal doesn't go through because it's your fault, like buyer's remorse. There are always devils in the details. They will have a memorandum of understanding sent shortly, with a contract shortly thereafter."

"Whoa! Slow down, Dwight. My head is spinning like a roof fan. Do they need all the money at close of escrow?"

"Yes, the owners said that was the only way they would sell the magazine, at seventy-five million dollars, with no annual payments. I guess I blurted out the higher amount to get it done. Sorry about that."

"Don't worry about that. What's another five million? I mean in the overall picture. And monthly payments with even 2 percent interest would be mind-boggling!"

"A couple of things, Blake. I want to hire an outside attorney and others to work with me just for the buyout, people who specialize in buyouts and mergers and the law involved in this kind of thing. They will cost extra. Probably at least one hundred thousand by the time this is over. Okay? The sellers will have their own top-notch attorneys, and they will try to take advantage of you. Money well spent."

"Sure. What else?"

"You should visit the other offices and get an idea of what you are buying. They will all be told you are a prospective buyer, and you should tell them their jobs are safe, unless you know differently."

"Actually, I really like most of the people we've got. I have only sparse knowledge about Chicago. More about New York. I've heard great things about them from my boss, who is the vice president and in charge of this office."

"In a couple of months, you will be his boss! Won't he be surprised?" asked Spenser.

"He sure will. But I may have some good surprises for them. Call me when you have something else."

"I will. That might be every day."

"Got it," said Blake. He left and looked at the magazine office in a completely different way. Then he drove to the *Register* office.

"Rex, can I see you and Liz?"

"Sure," said Rex, who was standing at the water cooler outside Liz's office. They all went into Rex's office. Blake shut the door.

"Rex, Liz, I'm going to buy SRM. I came into some money."

Both Rex and Liz couldn't say a word. Both just had their mouths open, waiting for the next shoe to drop.

"Rex, at the very least, you will keep your job with a substantial wage increase. Liz, I want you to train another secretary for Rex right away," said Blake.

"What? Don't you like my work?" asked Liz.

Blake liked teasing Liz, but it seemed to be a little cruel. "I am offering you a job as my personal assistant at double the salary. Yes, both of you are great, and I want you both to have a major part in the new *Sports Register Magazine.* Please don't mention my name or anything other than the magazine will be sold and will continue to operate—bigger and better! At some point, of course, we will tell everyone."

"So you want us to continue as we were? Okay, Blake, I need a story," said Rex.

"I will be working on that starting tomorrow," said Blake. "And, Rex, shut up! Liz, what are you thinking?"

"I'm speechless, Blake. Of course I would love to work for you, and, Rex, and I will look for another secretary. I appreciate you noticing that I am suitable to be much more in the magazine world."

"You will be working with me," said Blake. "You have been wonderful for years. I will be back in a couple of days to start some due diligence. If you have time, see what airlines fly to Chicago and New York and their schedules for next week, will you?"

"Of course, Blake. By the way, how did you come by all this money? And how much was it?"

"I won't tell you now, but the magazine is well funded."

"We both will be looking forward to working with you," said Rex. "I have some ideas I would like to run by you."

"We will have plenty of meetings in the near future. Get your ideas organized. I have to go now, but I will see you both soon."

As Blake walked out, one of the football writers accosted him. "Are you on vacation, Blake? I never see you anymore."

"Yeah, just taking it easy, Ed."

"Hey, you better step it up. The *Register* is going to be sold, and we have to impress the new owner."

"Yes, I know, Ed. I better get right on that."

Blake drove home and wanted to eat and rest his mind and body. This was just too much.

44

Blake left the next morning for the drive to Santa Ana for his meeting with Sheriff Blank Smith. He hadn't slept all night and started writing down all of his ideas so he wouldn't forget anything. He stopped at the desk in the public area and asked for Sheriff Smith. A young lady called his office and told Blake he would be right down. Instead, Pet came down and batted her eyes at Blake.

"I will take you up," said Pet. They left the lobby and walked to the elevator. Pet asked him how his night was. Blake was sure she was seducing him all the way up.

"Go right in, Blake. I will see you after you see the sheriff."

The sheriff opened the conversation. "Hello, Blake. Sit right down. I understand you came into some money, so to speak."

"I have a feeling you know how much exactly, Blank. What's on your mind?"

"I'm in the middle of that cheerleader murder. I'm at my wit's end. What do you think of it?"

This was the first time Blank didn't seem to be talking down to him. "Where are you?" asked Blank. "Are you going to remain working as a sports investigative reporter? I talked to the replacement cheerleader's parents. I didn't like them, but I just don't think they would murder someone. We interviewed the cheer advisor and school personnel, the replacement and other students. We are at a dead end."

"I'm in the same boat," said Blake. "I just don't know how I would act if someone intimated that I killed someone."

The sheriff answered, "But the mother had a reason to."

"You are only saying that because of that case in Texas years ago. You know, the one where the mother killed the cheerleader and her daughter stepped into the squad."

"You might be right. I called the sheriff in Texas and asked some questions. He could not prove the replacement knew her mother did it. He did prove the mother did it. I am going to interview the Nguyens tomorrow afternoon. Want to come?"

"Sure," replied Blake. "But I would like to look at the autopsy report."

"I wish I could do that, Blake. I'm afraid I would violate privacy laws, so I can't."

"That might help me a lot, Blank. Are you sure?"

"Yes. You have the Nguyens' address. I'll see you at three tomorrow."

As if on cue, Pet sauntered into the office and led Blake back to her office. "Oh, Blake, I have to go to the bathroom. Please don't look at the autopsy report on my desk and don't make copies, okay?"

As soon as Pet left, Blake made copies of the report and sat down. As if Pet had been watching, she came right in and sat at her desk.

"Sorry about that, Blake. Sometimes nature calls. What did Blank say?"

"Why do I think you know exactly what he wanted?" Blake didn't respond to her blank stare and asked when they could get together again.

"How about tomorrow night, after your visit to the Nguyens?" said Pet.

"How did you know I am going to visit them?"

"Just a bloody wild guess. Don't forget, Blank will meet you there and conduct the interview."

Blake smiled and walked out of her office holding ten sheets of paper in his right hand. He walked out of the building and went home. Time to read the autopsy report.

At home, Blake poured himself a caffeine-free Diet Pepsi, flopped down in his favorite recliner, and started to read about Rebecca Sterling. She was five- three, 110 pounds, and judging by the attached picture he had copied, she had been a pretty girl. She was found behind the main gym.

Her death was because of strangulation. She had marks on her neck that looked like some kind of barbed wire. And she had bruises on her face, and it looked like she had some defensive wounds on her arms and hands. It appeared she was overpowered by a strong person. Other items in the report supported the conclusion that she died of strangulation. She had not been sexually abused.

It looked to Blake like it was a strong, bigger person who did the job, or more than one person. The crime scene photos happened to be with the report, and it looked gruesome. But it gave Blake some answers. Should he thank Pet, not bring it up, or tell Pet to thank Blank? He'd have to think about that.

Blake called SRM to talk to Liz. "Hi, Liz. Set me up for the visits to the Chicago and New York offices the week after next. I need some time. I texted you the dates I can make it. Thank you."

Blake thought about the case for the next several hours. "What am I missing?" he said to no one but himself. "Who did this terrible thing?"

The next day, Blake was right on time. He rang the Nguyens' doorbell. He stepped inside and saw that Blank was already there with Pet. Vicki Nguyen was there along with her mother, Silvia Nguyen, a strange man, and a boy. Where was Vicki's dad, Robert Nguyen? Silvia Nguyen spoke first. "This is our attorney, Jack Lam. I thought it wise that he be here. Most of you know Vicki's friend, Johnny Mai."

Lam spoke up. "Why is this reporter here? I don't want him here."

"He is helping with the case," said the sheriff. "And what is this boy doing here?"

"I am here for moral support for Vicki," said Johnny, Vicki's 'boyfriend.'

"I don't need moral support," said Vicki.

"How about if Johnny and I wait outside? By the way, where is Mr. Nguyen?" asked Blake.

"That's fine," said Lam. "Mr. Nguyen could not break away from a business trip. We will call you as soon as he is available."

Johnny and Blake went into the backyard and sat on lawn chairs. The remaining people started talking. Blake started a conversation with Johnny.

"This is terrible you have to see this, Johnny. Boy, are you big? You play football?"

"It's a terrible thing that happened to Reb," said Johnny. "She and Vicki never really got along. They were in different groups. Some guys called it cliques. And I am a wrestler."

"Would that be gangs? Not groups or clubs?" asked Blake.

"We don't call them gangs. Just groups. Some call it a club. But one is Asian, and the other is not."

"I get it, Johnny. Could Vicki's group be involved in the murder?"

"Oh no. I'm in the same group as Vicki. We don't kill people. We call ourselves the Blades."

"Is there any way someone in your group could have been involved?"

"I just can't see that, mister, what was your name?"

"Mr. Brennon. Blake Brennon."

"Sometimes some of the members in different clubs get a little agitated, even fight a little, but not this."

"I can't seem to get a handle on your relationship with Vicki. Are you an item?"

"I thought we were, but since she became a cheerleader, she hasn't spoken to me much. She said I had to be here today to hear what was happening, but you and I got tossed."

"So what do you do at school besides homework?" asked Blake.

"I'm on the wrestling team. Top division."

"How are you doing?"

"Well, I'm on probation right now. I have to get my grades up."

"Good luck, Johnny. Nice talking to you."

"I hope it's the last time. I don't like all of this."

"Me too, Johnny." Blake got up and went inside. "Hey, Blank, done already?"

"Mrs. Nguyen keeps thinking I am accusing her of something. She is very defensive. Wants her husband to be here the next time if I have to talk to her."

"There shouldn't be a next time, Mrs. Nguyen," said Lam.

Blake, Blank, and Pet walked to their cars. Blake looked back to see Vicki dismissing Johnny. Johnny wasn't happy about it.

"They didn't come up with anything. The lawyer did the talking, and they twisted every word I said," said Blank.

"Pet, what did you get out of this?"

"Nothing. Vicki just sat there like a statue."

Blake thought Pet had more to say, but he would save that for when they were alone.

"Maybe I have something," Blake started. "Rebecca and Vicki were in separate gangs. Vicki's in the Blades, and they were rivals to Rebecca's gang, or club."

"I know about the Blades. Not the worst gang around, but we have had trouble," said Blank.

"I think you should talk to the Blades, and that includes Vicki. I will follow up with Johnny. Maybe he knows more than he told me. I think he does."

"Okay, Blake. Will do. Talk to you soon," said Blank as he walked away.

"Call me," said Pet as she followed the sheriff.

"Will do. Soon!"

Blake left and again looked back at the Nguyens' house. Vicki and Johnny had disappeared behind the side of the house. Silvia Nguyen was looking through the living room drapes at him. What was going on?

45

Blake got into his BMW, started back to his office, and didn't answer his ringing cell phone. When he got there, he found a place to park. He jotted down on his to-do list to get his name on a parking place. He looked at his phone and saw most of the messages were from Liz. He went to the *Register*'s eleventh floor and walked straight to Liz.

"Hi, Liz. Looking for me?"

"Yes. I have your tickets booked next week for Chicago and New York. I also booked you in nice hotels. I emailed you the itinerary and notified the *Register* offices you are coming. I just booked you for one full day at each office. If you want to change anything, let me know."

"Thanks, Liz. Now set up a meeting here for Friday afternoon. I sure don't want this office to be left out of the loop. In the meantime, see what information you can get on the Blades, a gang in Westminster. Call

Petula at the sheriff's office if you need help. I've got a hunch."

"Will do," said Liz. "By the way, I have an idea for my replacement for Rex's secretary. Maria Constantine. She's been in support here for fifteen years, and Rex likes and endorses her."

"Thanks, Liz. I will talk to her and let you know."

Blake walked out and just happened to walk past Maria's cubicle. She was about fifty, slim, and very neat and presentable. "Hi, Maria. How's it cooking?"

"Fine, Blake. Or do I have to call you Mr. Brennon now?" Great. Another person who already knew.

"No way. We've known each other the whole time you've been here. Are you happy here?"

"Of course, Blake. I've had regular pay raises, so I guess Rex likes my work."

Blake had always been impressed with Maria. She did everything. She helped in editing and story ideas and backed up Liz, who backed up Rex and reporters.

"Well, I just want to tell you your job is 100 percent safe, Maria. I know you've done a great job, and I have interacted with you for a long time. And you will be getting a special raise soon."

"Thank you, Blake. I really appreciate this. You don't know."

"Take care, Maria. I will talk to you soon."

Blake walked into Rex's office. They chatted about

things for fifteen minutes, and then Blake asked him about Maria. "I understand you endorse her being your right-hand person."

"I do. Since you're taking away the best employee you have, except me, she would make a great replacement."

"I think so too, Rex. You go hire her. Give her Liz's office after you find two suitable offices for Liz and me. Give her a 25 percent raise and explain to her how important her job is. I want to sit down with you in two weeks to go over your job description. It will be the same, running this office, including the Los Angeles publication of the *Register*. I will have you help me run this whole company too, so tell me what you will need to do that. BTW, give yourself a 25 percent raise too." (Each area of the country had their different publication. Many of the stories and departments were the same, but the covers and some of the stories inside were different.)

"BTW?" asked Rex. "You are really into this digital slang, huh? I will and thanks."

"We all have to get into it more. Like it or not, if we want to survive, we have to raise the bar for our emagazine. One of the things we are going to do is publish the paper version bimonthly, from weekly. The emag can change daily. Paper *Sports Illustrated* has gone to monthly. But they have a good digital mag. Give that some thought, will you?"

"You don't want me to sleep nights, do you?"

"You? Think about me! You remember those old spinning tops we used to play with when we were kids? Well, that's my head. But we're going to make this a very viable enterprise. One that sports fans will love to read. And before I forget, many girls and women are really getting into sports nowadays. Make sure they are now included in our demographics."

"I know," said Rex. "I have some ideas on that too."

"Wonderful. Not now. Let's close escrow first. But just think, our subscriber pool just went up 50 percent! Take care, Rex. BTW, I'm still working the cheerleader story."

"Great. Bye, boss."

"Don't boss me. We all have to pull this train, or it goes off the track. See you Friday. I asked Liz to get everyone together. Please coordinate with her to get everyone in this office here."

"Will do, boss." Rex smiled.

Blake went home to crash on his sofa. He thought about getting a more comfortable one, but that was fleeting. He had to think about eating and what to say to his Orange County office.

Spenser called Blake and told him the deal to purchase the *Register* magazine should close the following week. His office said the deal was very straightforward. Spenser said he would go over it at least two more times, as well as his other council he hired. He told Blake to put $75 million into escrow. Blake did. Blake had never written a check for $75 million before. He had to look it over a few times. He took it to the escrow office and rushed back home. Now, back to his meeting notes for tomorrow.

Blake found a place to park at the *Sports Register Magazine* office. It reminded him *again* to get a marked parking place. He saw the assembled group and started talking.

"As you all probably know, I just bought this magazine. I will let all of you know who will be staying within a month. The people I have to let go will get good severance pay. I will be honoring the pension plan for the time being and will actually better it soon. I know all of you well. A lot of you have been here as long as I have, fifteen years.

"You will know a lot more about my plans for the near future. Suffice to say, I plan to expand the company to include what amounts to a daily emagazine. We will go to a bimonthly paper magazine starting next month. That changes things a bit, and we will concentrate on sports humor and player profiles. But we can have timely news in the daily emag. Readers want to know more about the players they are rooting for. Good and bad!

"I'm sorry I can't tell you more. It's just that I don't know more at this time—except that Mr. Harrington will continue the run this office and help me run the whole company from this office. This office will be the home office starting next month. Please don't mention any of this to the other two offices, as I will be informing them next week. Any questions?"

Blake got the usual barrage of questions about seniority and job concerns. He tabled most of them but did address seniority. "I've never valued seniority over talent and attitude. I will keep the talented and loyal people. Just being here a long time doesn't cut it. I know I would never want to be anywhere unless I was an asset to them. I hope you all understand. This magazine will only survive with the best people at their jobs, doing the best they can. Including me."

Blake dismissed everyone and went into Rex's office. "It appears everyone took it well. What did you think?"

"I think so. I know you know we have a good crop of people here. I am putting together a confidential list of employees and my opinion of them. I also have here some notes on other employees in New York and Chicago for your trip next week. They are expecting you, and Liz has your itinerary and reservations."

"Thank you, Rex," said Blake before he headed to Liz's office.

"Here is everything you will need," said Liz. "By the time you get back, our offices will be set up, and we can go from there. By the way, Mr. Spenser called and said he should have the final papers for you to sign by the end of next week."

"Thank you, Liz. What a day. I'm going home to rest this weekend."

"No, you aren't, Blake. Is it okay if I still call you Blake?"

"Of course. Why not?"

"Petula called and said she will be sitting on your sofa when you get home."

"How does she get into my home? I know what her answer will be."

Blake left the building and drove home. Blake asked Pet the question. "How did you get in?"

"I am a detective, Blake. Can you get in places? Don't answer that. Anyway, sit down here, and I'll give you a massage."

Blake thought that sounded good. But as usual, the conversation turned to business. At least it was while she was rubbing his shoulders. "Blank said we should look into the Blades. He said maybe it was a tit-for-tat murder, so to speak."

"I thought of that," said Blake. "But they are a young group. Could they do that?"

"Blank asked the gang control group in our office, and they said the Blades have beaten some people up. Could be. We have to look into this," said Pet.

"By the way, what's this we thing?" asked Blake.

"He knows you want to help. And we need help on this one."

"Okay, tell him to interrogate the gang members and let me know. I won't be back until the end of next week."

"He's already started on that, but he wants you to interrogate Vicki. The one who replaced Rebecca. He can't get anything from them. Maybe you can. Blank thinks they look very suspicious."

"Yeah, I will. And yes, I still consider the Nguyen family as suspects, and the Blades too. Maybe even Vicki herself."

"Okay, Blake. Enough talk. Take you clothes off for an all-over massage," said Pet.

He did. She did.

Pet fled the next morning, so Blake had time to read his itinerary for the following week. Liz booked him into the Marriott Marquis in New York on Monday and Tuesday, because he would be meeting with the New York office on Tuesday. Then off to Chicago on Wednesday, staying at the Waldorf Astoria on Wednesday and Thursday nights, for a meeting with Chicago on Thursday. Back home Friday.

He was just contemplating all of this when his cell phone rang. "Hi, Blake. This is Liz. Vicki Nguyen just called and wants to talk to you."

"Tell her I would love to talk to her but make it for a week from Monday at my office."

"She wants to meet you in Westminster. She doesn't feel comfortable anywhere else. She said come alone. She has information you will want."

"Okay, Liz. Ask if she can make it about ten next Monday."

"Okay, Blake. Did you get the tickets and itinerary?"

"Yes, I did," answered Blake. "Please tell the other offices I will be there. Have them send cars to pick me up at the hotel at least one hour before the meeting times. Ask them to have all employees there, if possible."

"The cars are already set up, to and from. By the way, your meeting here went great. Everyone really felt enthused."

"Great to hear, Liz. I'm going to get ready this weekend. I will call you during the week. Don't forget to call Vicki."

"Got it, Blake. Have a good trip. If you need anything, you have all my numbers."

"I sure do. Thanks, Liz."

Blake was wondering why Vicki wanted to talk to him, but right now he had to develop two good speeches. He knew many of the other employees, but now he was just about the owner of the *Sports Register Magazine*. They would be looking to him not only for ideas but to keep their jobs. It was not a position Blake liked to be in.

46

Blake boarded a United plane and took it to New York. Liz had made first-class reservations. Blake didn't think he needed that. He would tell her later. But he enjoyed the attention and food and unlimited diet drinks. Maybe he wouldn't mention it. Blake worked on his speeches.He called the flight attendant over: "Another Diet Pepsi please!"

Blake got off in New York and took a taxi to the Marriott Marquis. It was a modern hotel. He was impressed. Very nice. His room was even nicer—queen bed, desk, two chairs, and a big TV.

He put down his paperwork, unpacked his bags, and then noticed it was late. *That three-hour time difference!*

Blake worked on the finishing touches of his talk, looked over the names at the New York location to at least remember the names of the people he should remember, and then got a call from a lawyer.

"Mr. Brennon? I am George Snodgress. I am affiliated with the firm that is helping you with the contract to buy the *Sports Register Magazine*. I have it here. I can be at your hotel room in thirty minutes for you to sign it. Mr. Spenser said it looked good."

"Okay. It's kind of late. Drop it by, and then if it looks good, I will sign it, and you can meet me at the New York office of SRM tomorrow after ten to pick it up. I will tell them you are coming."

"SRM?"

"Yes. *Sports Register Magazine*. Sorry about that," said Blake.

George Snodgrass dropped it off, gave Blake his card, and told Blake he would see him the next day. It was after midnight. Blake looked it over, texted Dwight Spenser, his attorney, and decided to leave it to Dwight and his posse to read the fine print.

By early the next morning, Dwight Spenser replied and told Blake to sign it. If he did, he would be the official owner that day.

Blake signed it, wondering what he was getting into, and put it in his briefcase. With that, he was called and told his car was waiting. Blake went down after putting on his best suit and tie and taking his briefcase.

The car took him to an older but well-kept building near Macy's. The *Register* had the bottom three floors. He went to the third floor.

He approached the receptionist. "Hello, my name is Blake Bren—"

"Yes, Mr. Brennon. Dan Alexander is expecting you. Walk this way."

This was more formal than Orange County. Everyone looked like they were going to a premier red carpet show or something.

"Hello, Blake," said Dan. "We've known each other for years. Should I call you Mr. Brennon?"

"No, no, Dan. I know this is strange. You are my boss one day and work for me the next. But I know you well, and I want you to know right now that your position is yours. I will need limited SRM resumes and your opinion of everyone else. I will rely on your recommendations on their employment status."

"Thank you, Blake. Have you given any thought to the future?"

"Yes, a lot. But we only have an hour before the meeting, right? Show me around, then I'll talk at the meeting, and then you can take me to lunch. On the expense account of course. By the way, you will be getting a raise."

"Wonderful and thank you. I've already made a reservation at the View Restaurant in your hotel. It revolves and advertises culinary excellence. We take team owners and major sports stars there. Excellent food," said Dan.

"Kinda funny, huh, Dan? I've had more than few

meals with you. Mostly hotdogs. Now we are having culinary excellence. Next time I visit, take me to a good pastrami place. But this is good now. We have some things to talk about in private."

"Sure thing, Blake. Okay, this is my office ..."

Dan showed Blake around. Really, the offices were much like those in Orange County, only there was more room given to digital. Everyone was very well dressed, as opposed to Orange County, but that could be because Blake was going to address them pretty soon.

It was 10:00 a.m., time to address about thirty people, men and women of all ages.

Dan Alexander spoke first: "Ladies and gentlemen, here is the future owner of the *Sports Register Magazine*."

Just then, Blake saw George Snodgrass through the conference room window. Blake waved him in. He said a few words and then gave him the signed document. Snodgrass left, and Blake whispered something to Dan, who then said, "Excuse me, ladies and gentlemen. I would like to introduce you to the new owner of the *Register*, Mr. Blake Brennon."

The crowd gave him a lukewarm welcome, and he started to talk.

"I know this is a nervous time for all of you. Let me first say that you will be evaluated, especially by Dan. If you are thinking of retiring or moving on, please tell Dan by tomorrow. And no, if you got drunk with me in the past, that will not be held against you. And yes, I still don't drink, but you still can.

"As you all know, magazines are fading. We used to have ten million subscribers, and now we have five. So why did I buy this magazine? The digital form is taking off. We will start printing just twice a month, but we will be a digital emagazine ready to change some things daily. We must figure out a better way to tell our younger prospective subscribers we are available. This will mean we need more employees, not less."

The crowd gave him enthusiastic applause.

"A lot of us are resistant to change. Me too. But we must do this to stay a viable market for sports news in this century. We will do even more human interest stories. Fans really like knowing what's happening in the personal lives of everyone involved. Even sportswriters. They want to know how sports impacts their cities. They want to know why an NFL quarterback gets twenty million dollars a year and a rocket scientist teacher gets a hundred and fifty thousand. There are reasons. We must show them. Good and bad. That is our job."

Blake got an even heartier applause.

"In short, ladies and gentlemen, there is great opportunity here. A lot more than if we tried to just stay a paper magazine. I am enthused. And you are the very first to know officially I am the new owner. We can do it. But only as a team. There is no I in team. But as the late basketball player Kobe Bryant said, 'Yes, but there is an m-e, and I intend to be here right with you!'"

Everyone stood and cheered. Blake was really happy.

"I want you all to know that Dan Alexander will stay on as your manager, and I am giving him a title of vice president. I really expect this office to contribute a great deal to the *Sports Register Magazine*. I hope we will all prosper. By the way, if any of you want to make suggestions, go through Dan. If you feel he isn't available, you can call me.

"Also, the home office will be moved to Orange County, so you will have even more space in these offices. I might reduce the space to two floors, but we'll see when the lease expires. But you will have plenty of room. Please refer any questions to Dan. I just can't answer any questions now since I've only been the owner for about a half hour. It was a pleasure seeing all of you. Most of you I know, and I'll be back with more answers in the near future. In the meantime, keep doing what you're doing. This is a great sports magazine. I hope we all can make it greater."

Dan and Blake went directly to the elevator to a round of applause. The same car took Blake and Dan to the View Restaurant. Dan told Blake that it went very well, and he looked forward to pushing the magazine to the top.

The two sat down at a nice table overlooking the city

of New York from all sides, as the view was seen from a spectacular revolving restaurant.

"That seemed to go well, huh, Dan?" asked Blake.

"Very well. I liked how you glossed over the bimonthly thing and emphasized the digital move."

"Give that some thought, Dan. How can we entice the readers to read it? That will make the advertisers want to advertise. Hire a consultant for that purpose. We have to move on that."

"I will, Blake. I didn't realize you were going to change the home office to LA."

"Sorry about that, Dan. But now you won't have the brass breathing down your neck. Remember how you hated that? You told me a number of times."

Dan was embarrassed. "Boy, be careful who your talking to, right, Blake? I didn't really mean it."

"Yeah, right. I didn't like the oversight by Rex Harrington, my Orange County, or as you say, LA, counterpart. In any event, I am counting on you to hold this up. That's why you are a vice president. By the way, don't tell Rex. I will be making him an executive vice president. What do you think about Al Snook, the Chicago manager?"

"I'd rather wait until you meet him. He is different. Maybe a short-timer. I know you don't know him well," said Dan.

"Okay. Hold off on your VP announcement for a week or so. Okay, Dan?"

"I will."

Blake and Dan finished their lunch talking about a few things and were sipping on a Diet Coke and margarita.

"So, Blake. How's your love life?" asked Dan. "I know that Rhino cheerleader's death was really hard on you, especially after you dated her. Great series of articles though."

"Yes, she was a nice girl. Not really a relationship though. I'm dating a sheriff deputy now."

"A sheriff? Does she have a gun?" asked Dan.

"Yes, I really like her. She's the most beautiful woman I've ever seen. And very sexy. But I just can't seem to trust her, although she seems to admit it when she's pumping me for information."

"And you get information from her?"

"As much as I can."

"So just keep going until you figure out she's the one for you. Don't worry about it now. You have enough going on."

"That I do, Dan. I'm going up to my room. Nice to see you. I will be in touch. Don't forget to call that digital consultant."

With that, Dan left and Blake went up to his room. It had been a good day. Almost lost in everything was that Blake now was the sole owner of the *Sports Register Magazine*.

The next morning, Blake was picked up for his trip

to the airport. He landed in Chicago. He didn't know a lot of people there, as he normally visited New York on his sports travels.

There was no car to pick him up as arranged. He caught a cab and drove to the Waldorf Astoria, a quaint, old but elegant hotel not far from the Chicago *Register* office.

Blake called the Chicago *Register*. "Hello. Al Snook please."

"This is Mr. Snook's office," replied the secretary. "You want Mr. Snook? Who's calling?"

"This is Blake Brennon. Please put him on."

"Mr. Brennon," said Snook. "Did the car come for you?"

"No. I took a cab. I will expect a car to pick me up tomorrow morning early, for our meeting and to address the employees."

"Yes, of course, Mr. Brennon. I can't figure out where that car is. I'll find out."

"Fine, Al. By the way, get me a plane out of Chicago tomorrow evening. I don't want to wait for the next morning. I would like to meet with you at a restaurant close to the airport after our meeting with the troops. Okay?"

"Yes, Mr. Brennon. It will be taken care of."

Blake didn't quite like the conversation. It made him rethink his talk for tomorrow, and he had another idea that he was thinking about even before this conversation.

Blake couldn't sleep much that night. The next morning, he packed his bags because he was going home that night, right from his talk.

The car picked him up, and they went to the *Register* office, which was on two floors of an old Chicago building. It was close to the Loop and not far from Wrigley Field. Blake had been there a few times, but the Cubs and White Sox had been covered well by this office over the years.

The car dropped him off, and Blake went up to the tenth floor. He found out Snook was on the eleventh floor. No one escorted him up there, but Blake got finally got seated in front of Al Snook. Snook was a long-timer, about sixty-five years old. Bald and fat. Just like Blake remembered.

"Hi, Al. How's it going?"

"Good, Mr. Brennon. When are you taking us over?"

"Yesterday," said Blake. "I know the meeting starts soon. Please show me around. It looks a lot different from when I was here last."

Snook showed Blake around. Some of the people he knew, but apparently there had been a pretty big turnover in the last year.

"Where is your digital department, Al?"

"Oh, we have a person over by the window. But, Mr. Brennon, you and I don't like digital, do we? You are going to go big-time with the magazine, right?"

"You are partially right, Al. I dislike digital. But we are going to go down to twice a month on the magazine and go whole hog on the digital. It's not what I want; it's what we have to do to keep up with what the public demands. Capisce?"

"I don't know, Mr. Brennon. I just don't know if I can do this. It just isn't right."

"It may not be right, but it's what we are going to do, and soon. Can you continue to captain this ship?"

"I will try, Mr. Brennon. But my heart really isn't in it."

"I appreciate your honesty. I have made a decision I was going to put off for a while. I will tell you and the rest of the people at our meeting. Thank you, Al."

They went into the conference room. About twenty people were there. Blake started to talk. "First, I want to thank all of you for the good job you have done here for years. It is hard when a lot of changes have to be made. I don't like it, but I must do some things I don't like.

"Effective next month, I will be closing this branch of the *Sports Register Magazine*. We will have a presence here of probably two people in a small office in Chicago. Mr. Snook, I think that you deserve to retire with full benefits. Most of you will be offered jobs in Orange County, known as LA to most of you, or New York.

"The salaries should be the same, and I will help with moving expenses. I will also have nice severance packages for those of you who terminate. For the rest of this month, you will work half-time but be paid for full time. You will work out a schedule with Mr. Snook. I need you to have a notice of your intentions, including where you want to work, on Mr. Snook's desk Monday morning. I'm sorry to have to report this to you, but it's the sign of the times. We must move forward or perish.

"Please direct any questions to Mr. Snook. Please give him your intentions by Monday morning.

"Mr. Snook, I will call you Tuesday after you fax their intention sheets to me in Orange County, and that will be the new home office.

"Mr. Snook, please drive me to the airport."

Snook drove Blake to the restaurant on way to the airport in silence. The office employees and Snook said nothing. Blake felt terrible but knew it was the right thing to do.

Snook had made a reservation at the Loop Restaurant. He and Blake sat down.

"Well, that was some speech," said Snook. "I could see me going. I was going to retire when it was good for you anyway."

"I'm sorry, Al. I will plan on you handling everything. I'm sure all of that will take place through the end of next month. I know I said this month. If you handle everything smoothly, there will be a bonus for you as well as honoring your pension."

"I understand, Blake. I have to get back to try and soothe some ruffled feathers. I will talk to you on Monday."

"Thank you, Al. In addition, I need an honest, private letter on each employee and your estimate on how they could do in the future in this new environment, including their past history. That's very important. You've been in this business a long time. Your input is valuable!"

"I will do that, Blake. I know what I will be doing this weekend."

Snook left Blake at the restaurant, and the car took him back to the office. Blake took a cab to the airport. He didn't feel quite as bad as he thought he would. He thought he had treated everyone fairly. He sure hadn't gotten the same vibe from that office as he had from the other two, but maybe it was him. He wanted to keep the good employees, the good writers.

Blake finally boarded the plane to Orange County Airport. He slept the whole way.

47

It was nice to be back in Orange County, California. Blake didn't have much time to figure out where he was going to go from there, but he called Liz. "Liz, am I set up for Vicki Monday?"

"You sure are, Blake. She wants to meet you at 1211 Main Street in Westminster. I don't recognize the address."

"Okay. She only weighs about a hundred pounds. I should be able to handle her."

Blake rested the balance of the weekend, and then Monday came around. So Blake drove out to Westminster and parked in front of something that looked like a clubhouse he used to play in as a kid. He was a little apprehensive but approached the front door and knocked. Vicki answered the door.

"Hello, Mr. Brennon. Come in."

"What is this place?" asked Blake.

"This is our clubhouse. Have a seat."

Blake sat on an old sofa, just like the one he used to sit on back in his high school sports club.

"Now, what is it you want to tell me, Vicki?" asked Blake as he put a small digital recorder on a box that doubled as a coffee table. "I want to get this down. We are being recorded."

Then seven boys, looking like late teens, came in from another room, carrying knives.

"Stay seated, Mr. Brennon," said the tall, skinny guy named Rats. He was apparently the ringleader. "We want you to stop investigating the cheerleader murder."

"Why? Did you guys do it?"

"No, we didn't, but you are harassing Vicki. She is a good member of our club, and it makes us look bad."

Just then, a familiar figure came to the front. It was Vicki's boyfriend.

"Well, hello, Johnny. What is this all about?" asked Blake.

"Rats just told you. You are making Vicki and her family nervous. Her parents don't even want Vicki to see me because of you."

"It's not just me. The police are on it too. By the way, I'm taping everything so I don't miss anything."

"The police have talked to us. You must be feeding them. We want you to stop investigating us and tell the police we are not suspects," growled Johnny.

"And, Mr. Brennon, you won't need that tape recorder." Rats stepped on it over and over again with big, heavy boots.

"I don't like being threatened. If I don't quit the case, you will carve me up, right?" said Blake.

"No, you will voluntarily stop it right now."

"Why would I do that?" asked Blake.

Just then, Vicki tore her blouse and started screaming. She threw herself on Blake. Blake instinctively held her and tried to get her off of him. It took him a few minutes to do that. About that time, several of the guys in the room came and separated Blake from Vicki. They tenderly sat a crying Vicki on a chair and threw Blake down.

"What are you doing, Vicki?" asked Blake. He noticed Johnny was taking pictures or a video of the altercation with his cell phone.

Johnny chimed in. "Why did you try to assault Vicki? It's a good thing we just came in. And I got it on tape too," said a very sarcastic Johnny.

Vicki was still crying. It looked like she was playing actress for the cell phone.

"What is going on?" asked Blake.

The skinny guy, Rats, spoke up. "I tell you what, Mr. Brennon. I think we can keep this from the police and your boss at the *Register*. Would you like that?"

"What do you want from me?" asked Blake.

"You are done with your investigation. You will never talk to anyone here or Vicki's parents or friends about this. Right, Mr. Brennon?"

Blake took a moment to decide what to say. Obviously, the gang didn't know about his recent fortune. What was he going to do? On top of that, these were just kids—twenty at the oldest. How would he handle it? Blake needed more time.

"I guess you got me," said Blake. "I don't want to be arrested or fired from my job. I'll back off."

Vicki and the boys all smiled like THEY had just won the lottery. Johnny held up the cell phone, and the rest pushed Blake out the front door. Vicki had stopped crying and was laughing. What an actress. Blake got in his BMW and went straight to the sheriff's office.

He barged right into Blank's office.

"You'll never guess what happened!" said Blake. Blake told him the entire story. "I think I should appear to be backing off. I can tell you what gives. Give me a day or two to think this through, and we can form a plan."

"You come back, and we'll form a plan," said Blank. "They were really dumb to do this. They weren't on my radar. In fact, no one was. How stupid can they be?"

"They're just kids but with adult toys and a gangster mentality. That will work to our advantage."

"Okay, Blake. But I don't know what pictures they have. You went to her clubhouse, and she will testify against you for attempted rape. The scumbags will be witnesses. You have to take that into consideration. We are being pressured to prosecute cases just like this!"

"I understand, Blank. And I agree. The Blades just jumped to number one on my suspect list too. Let's get 'em!"

Blank thought for a minute. "It's too bad they took your recorder. That would stop 'em!"

"They didn't take my recorder. They took an old cell phone that didn't even work. But I do have my recorder pens in my pocket. In fact, two of them. A reporter always carries at least two pens in case one stops working!"

"You are a genius, Blake. But in California, both parties have to know they are being taped, or it's inadmissible."

"Oh, I told all of them. They just smashed the wrong recording device. Not my fault."

Blake visited with Pet and set up a later date. Right now, he had a lot on his plate. A whole lot. He got in his car and went home.

Blake called his attorney, Dwight Spenser, and asked him to meet him on Saturday at Spenser's office.

Saturday came. "Hi, Dwight," said Blake. "I want to discuss my new business. I don't want to run the everyday activities. I want to make big final decisions, but I want to just write my stories like I used to, though I will decide what and when."

"You can do that, Blake. Pick someone to run the

show, make yourself chairman of the board, and you call the shots after you set the culture and goals. No problem," said Spenser.

"Okay. Set up everything to do this and tell me next week what I need to do."

"Sure, Blake. But I have bad news."

"What is it?"

Spenser handed Blake the new issue of the *Inquisiter*, the number one gossip magazine in the world. It had a picture of Blake on the cover, showing Blake as a lottery winner and new owner of the *Sports Register Magazine*. "That rock don't roll," said Blake. "No one contacted me."

"They contacted me. I said no comment," said Spenser.

"If they call back, confirm just those two items. A million people know about it. It could be anyone. And it may be no coincidence that the *Inquisiter* has its home office in Chicago. I just closed that office."

"Has the fun started yet, Blake? I'm sorry. It seems like a lot. I have another member of your legal team spending more time in my office than his. I might bring him here with me full-time. Anyway, I will start him on everything Monday. I may have to call you a lot for a while."

"Thanks, Dwight. I may have to live here too. Hope not. Call me anytime you need to. You have my numbers. Gotta go. Have a date with Pet. Bye."

Blake drove home and waited for Pet to arrive. As

usual, she arrived a bit late and looking like the gorgeous woman that she was. Breathtaking would be the word. And very sexy too. Even more than ever.

"Hi, gorgeous. Come on in."

"Hi, Blake," she said. "Are you ready to go out and eat?"

"I can't take you out like that. Too many people will gawk at you."

"I can handle it. You wouldn't believe I have a gun hidden on me, would you?"

"You can show me where when we get back. But I really can't believe it. Do you want me to pack the gun for you?"

"No, I'm comfortable. So, wine and dine me, and then let's get back!"

Blake and Pet went to the Ritz, a fancy restaurant in Newport Beach. As they entered the valet area, Blake and Pet noticed a huge gathering of people surrounding the entrance of the Ritz. When he exited his car with Pet, it seemed like a million lightflashes went off, and there were questions yelled at him from all over.

"What is going on, Pet?"

"It looks like your secret is out. People want to see the new *Register* owner and new lottery winner."

Restaurant employees cleared a path for them and sat them at a secluded table that overlooked the ocean. Blake realized the Ritz was prepared and had done this for celebrities. But how did the press know he was coming?

How could they have been prepared? How did they know? He wondered.

"Come on, Blake. You're a detective. Someone spilled the beans," said Pet.

"But who? And I just made the reservations yesterday. I better not use my name next time."

As Blake was looking at the throng of people outside the restaurant window, his mind came back to him. Pet was dressed unusually well. She had known where they were going. She discussed it at the sheriff's office. In fact, she had picked the place. But there were a lot of people who knew about Blake's windfall.

Blake decided to put it out of his mind and enjoy Pet. And there was a lot to enjoy. But then after they ordered, she started talking. "So, anything new on the cheerleader case?"

"I've been out of town, as you know. Did Blank fill you in?"

"Yes, as always. Are you going to continue, or are you too busy?"

"I am going to see this through. That gang did it, I'm sure. Or maybe just Vicki. But they sure don't seem like murderers. Close to it though."

"Good. We really need some help on this one. We just can't gain any traction. Blank figures you can get some answers. We have too many laws hampering us. You are a journalist but also licensed as a private eye. You can do a lot more digging. Please dig!"

"I'll dig," said Blake. "But right now, I want to dig into this food and pretend there aren't a hundred people watching us eat, if not more."

"Sure, Blake. Eat up. But hurry. I want to get you home."

Blake was mesmerized by Pet. No doubt about it. But he always wondered how much more to her there was. He always ended that thought with *I don't care.*

Blake and Pet exchanged some personal thoughts, but Pet impressed Blake with a special thought. Blake and Pet finished their dinner, fought through the crowd, got in the BMW, and went to Blake's condo. Little did he know what would be forthcoming. Little did he know.

The next morning, Blake followed Pet to work at the sheriff's office. Pet led Blake right into Blank's office. Blank was obviously expecting him.

"Hi, Blake," said Blank. "I guess you have a plan for my cheerleader case?"

"Pretty much. But first I need a bodyguard. Not only because of the Blades, but you should have seen us at dinner last night. Pure bedlam!"

"Got it," replied Blank. "I have two agencies that employ ex-cops. They are very good. I put my contact names on the list I'm handing you."

Obviously, Pet had relayed some pillow talk to Blank. "Thank you, Blank, and obviously Pet."

"Now," said Blank. "What do we do next?"

"You used to tell me. Now you're asking me?"

"This is a puzzler. The board of supervisors is on my ass—excuse my language, Petunia. I really need to do something," said Blank, still calling her Petunia.

"Okay. Give me a day to get protection, and you talk to Vicki. Rattle her. Bring her parents in. Talk to some of the gang members. Let's stir up the hornets' nest."

"I was thinking along those same lines. I'll do it today. But it might put you in danger."

"I would not run before all this, and I won't run now. Let's do it. It's the principle of the thing. And please wait until tomorrow. Now, which one of these protection services do you like best?"

"Go to Intertec. Joe Sampson. I'll call him and tell him you're on your way. Pet, you go back to work. Let's do it."

48

Blake waved goodbye to Pet like they were just friends and drove to Intertec. It was a very nice office building close to the sheriff's office in Santa Ana. Blake went in and saw the receptionist.

"You must be Mr. Brennon," said the very nice-looking, redheaded young lady. She buzzed Joe Sampson and escorted Blake into a lavish office with pictures of police officers on the walls.

"Come, sit down," said Joe Sampson. "I've heard all about you from Sheriff Smith. I hear you want protection."

"Well," said Blake, "I want to talk about it. What do you know about me? Do you know my secret?"

"You mean about the lottery? Don't worry. I won't jack up my fee too much."

"Yes, now tell me about your agency."

"All ex-cops that left the forces are in very good

standing. They all carry weapons and are well trained. Do you want twenty-four-hour protection?"

"I think I will try sixteen-hour protection for now. When can I meet your choice for my guard?"

Sampson buzzed the pretty redhead, and in a minute, Tim Anderson came in. Anderson was a really military-looking guy with a crewcut, not that muscular. He shook hands with Blake and sat beside him.

"Don't let my average size fool you, Mr. Brennon. I'm an expert in martial arts and can shoot my gun. I left the force because the money here is a lot more. But I help the police anytime I can. Any questions?"

Blake felt a bit rushed but did ask, "How can you handle sixteen hours a day, seven days a week?"

Sampson broke in. "He only does ten to twelve hours a day, six days a week. Our temporaries are very good and will spell Anderson at his discretion, depending on the circumstances of the day. Don't worry about overtime. Everything is included in our fee." He handed Blake an agreement. He could see why Anderson took the Intertec job. He signed it and asked Anderson when he would start.

"I'm following you home right now. It starts right now."

"Actually, I'm relieved. I've felt a bit threatened lately. I'll explain my situation when we get home."

"I know the thumbnail version, but I would like to know more," said Anderson.

The two of them drove to Blake's home. While inside, Blake told Anderson the whole story and agreed to tell Anderson in advance all of his plans. Right now, it was a trip to SRM.

"Hello, Rex. I asked Liz to sit in. This is Tim Anderson, my protector. I mean my escort. That sounds even worse. Anyway, here is what's going down.

"You, Rex, are now the CEO of SRM. The home office will be here. You are grooming a man who will manage the Orange County office. Yes, I know it is the LA office, but now it's the Orange County office, serving LA. I am closing the Chicago office. Employees that want to will be considered for transfer to here or New York. Chicago's Al Snook will be sending you the list of his employees who want to go or transfer. You make the decisions and then see me before the final decisions. You work out the details of the assignments for the different offices. I would like it to be operational by the end of next month. Any questions?"

"Yes. I hope you wrote all that down."

"Yes I did, Rex. It's on your cell phone."

"Good. What are you going to do?" asked Rex.

"I want to continue to write stories for the *Register.* Only, I will decide what to write, and your editors will all think the stories are great, and you will publish them. Okay?"

"I don't think that will ever be a problem. You are the

best writer in the country. I just never told you that to keep you on your toes," admitted Rex.

"I know. That's one reason you are the CEO. We will have many meetings. You will be on my board, and I will be chairman of the board, stacked with my people. You are one of them. I put a fortune into this venture, and I want to make sure it at least breaks even."

"It will do better than that," said Rex. "I have space in our offices so you and Liz can have all the room you need."

"Good. Liz, here has a long list of things I need done. We'll go to your office and discuss it."

Liz, Blake, and Anderson walked a few steps to Liz's office. "Nice digs, Liz. When did you fix this up?" asked Blake.

"The week you were back east," she said. "Let's see that list."

"As you can see, Liz, you are the owner's executive assistant. And the buffer between people who want to see or talk to me. If in the future, if you need an assistant, see me."

"Okay, Blake. I will take care of everything on the list."

Blake walked into his office with Anderson and sat at the big desk. Anderson sat on the couch. Blake really felt like a big shot. Of course, he paid for it. It was time to formulate his plan to deal with the Blades and the murder. Blake felt a lot better with Anderson, but he would still be cautious.

Blake answered his cell phone. It was Blank. "Blake, I have Vicki and her parents coming tomorrow with their lawyer. You can sit behind the two-way mirror. Ten sharp."

"I'll be there, Blank. This should be interesting."

Blake was at the sheriff's station at 9:30. Blank set him up in the observation room that had coffee and a speaker so he could hear what was being said. Vicki, her parents, and the lawyer came in, unaware that Blake was listening.

Blank's side had Pet and a male detective, with Blank leading the interrogation.

"Mr. and Mrs. Nguyen, Vicki, Holmes, we have some troubling information that we have to get some answers to. We are going to find out who murdered Rebecca Sterling, and we will not leave any stone unturned."

"We understand, Sheriff, but you have to stop listening to that sportswriter, Blake Brennon. He's not a cop and shouldn't even be listened to."

"You don't see him here, do you? I go by the facts."

Attorney Holmes spoke up. "We do too, Sheriff. But nobody here had anything to do with the killing. We think it was deplorable. That's why we are here."

Blank said, "Good. All of you had a motive, with Vicki gaining the dream of her life, as she once said. Rebecca was killed at the school, so many people could have had the opportunity."

"But wasn't she strangled? You can't say she had the means," stated attorney Holmes.

"She was strangled, but Rebecca was small, just like Vicki, and the scuttlebutt is Vicki and Rebecca didn't like each other."

Vicki's mother, Silvia Nguyen, chimed in. "Vicki is very popular. We don't know what Rebecca did to get the final spot on the squad. All the girls seem to be competitive."

"But only Vicki was moved up, and Rebecca was killed. How competitive was Vicki? Or how competitive are her parents?" said Blank.

Silvia responded, "We had nothing to do with this, Sheriff. We all deeply resent this implication."

"We are not implying anything," said Blank. "But what about Vicki and the Blades kidnapping Blake Brennon and threatening him?"

The lawyer and Vicki's parents both stared at Vicki. Silvia piped up. "Vicki, you said Mr. Brennon came to visit you, and you asked him to stop harassing us. You said he agreed. Anything else?"

Vicki was on the verge on crying. "No, Mom, that's all!"

"What if I can prove he was threatened by Vicki and other club members?" asked Blank.

"That would be impossible," stammered Vicki. "I mean, there can't be proof because it didn't happen."

Blank said, "He said your boyfriend and others were there, and you said there would be consequences if he didn't stop."

"I didn't say anything," she said.

"But you just said you were alone with him."

"I was, but he attacked me," said Vicki.

"What?" asked Vicki's mother and father at the same time.

"Why didn't you tell us, Vicki?"

"I didn't want to get you in any deeper," said Vicki.

Blank spoke up. "Now, Vicki, are you telling me that you are accusing Mr. Brennon of attacking you? Will you sign a complaint against him?"

"No, nothing really happened, because he got scared and ran out. I just want this to end."

The attorney finally said, "Sheriff, we need to confer with Vicki."

"Sure, Counselor. I'll leave, and you just knock on the door when you are ready to come back."

Blank went around to the observation room and talked to Blake. "Blake, I've seen a lot of liars in my time, and a sixteen-year-old just doesn't have the capacity to pull this off. I think we have our murderer in her family somewhere."

"Yes, Blank. I agree. But I don't think any of them have the strength to strangle Rebecca."

"They could have hired someone or done it together."

"Yes, all that is possible," said Blake, "but did you see the looks on the lawyer's and Vicki's parents' faces when she said she was attacked by me?"

"Yes, and I'm not even going to tell them now that we have recorded proof of the whole meeting."

"Good. Let's see where this goes and go from there. I'll stay here with Anderson until they are out of sight," said Blake.

Blank went back into the interrogation room. "What did you decide?"

"We want more time to figure all this out," said attorney Holmes.

"Sure, but Mr. Nguyen, you haven't said anything."

"No. I am out of town a lot, and I just heard of this. But no one in my family killed anybody. My wife said she is suspected because somewhere else, another cheerleader's mother killed someone. That doesn't mean she did it."

"I never accused anyone of murder, but I sure don't like lies. Get your stories straight and let's see if that makes the rock roll!"

"What?" asked the lawyer.

"Mr. Brennon always said if 'that rock don't roll' there is something wrong. Right now all of your rocks don't roll."

"We will be in touch, Sheriff," said Holmes.

"You do that. Soon," said Blank. His two detectives

and Blank left the room. Blank went back again to see Blake.

"They know they are in trouble."

Blake looked puzzled. "I just don't think they did it. Something smells bad. Are the parents in on it? I just don't know."

"We'll see. I will call you when they are ready to talk. I won't give them too long."

"Thanks, Blank."

Blake waited a while and walked out to his car with Anderson. *What's next?* he thought.

Blake and Anderson drove to Blake's next appointment, his final medical appointment with Dr. Hart. *A good name for a heart doctor*, he thought.

"Hello, Doctor. I know you got a call from Sheriff Smith. I have a little problem, and I need your help. But you can't breathe a word. Might lose my job," said Blake.

"Yes, I know all about it," said Hart. "I need to get you into a cath lab, and I'll give you what you need. How about tomorrow?"

"Sounds good. At Hoag Memorial?"

"Yes. Do I need anything?" asked Blake.

"Just a ride home, and take it easy the rest of that day—and don't eat anything else today. I have everything I need for the procedure."

"I have a ride. He's sitting outside. Remember, mum's the word."

"Okay," said the doc. "By the way, did you know I can read?"

"Uh, I hope so."

"I know you won the lottery, own a magazine, and help the police. I just thought I would get that out of the way."

"Sorry," said Blake. "Please tell no one about my procedure. If anyone found out, my life could be endangered. Okay?"

"Sure. Only three-quarters of my office knows about it. Mum's the word."

Blake and Anderson left the doctor's office and drove home. Pet called, but he told her he would see her in a couple of days. He asked Anderson not to mention the heart procedure to anyone. It was important. Anderson agreed.

Anderson left in the early afternoon and was replaced by a gorilla of a man. Blake called him King Kong. Anderson arrived early the next day and drove Blake to Hoag Memorial Hospital. Blake was wondering when the sixteen-hour protection was going to start. It sure was twenty-four-hours now.

Anderson waited in the waiting room while Blake was wheeled into the pre-op department.

Dr. Hart came in. "Okay, Mr. Brennon. You are set to go. We'll fix up that artery in no time. Any questions?"

"No, just get me through this."

Doctor Hart said there was nothing to it and promised good results. Blake didn't remember what he said, as he was sound asleep before he knew it. Blake woke up a couple of hours later. The first people he saw in the recovery room were Anderson, Blank, and Pet.

"How are you?" they seemed to ask in unison.

"I'm great."

"I'm glad you told me about this in my office," said Blank. "I then told Pet, but she already knew."

"Pillow talk," admitted Blake. "But I'm glad you're here."

"Glad to be here." Pet smiled. "But don't worry. I'll kiss it better."

"Okay, but again, people. Nobody can know!"

Pet said, "We know. Like you said, no big deal. You're going home soon. It's just an outpatient thing. I'll follow you home. Anderson doesn't have to babysit you any more today." Blake went home. Blank went back to his office.

"Anderson, go get lunch, will you?" said Blake.

"Sure," said Anderson. "You look like you are in good hands. See you in a couple."

Pet pushed Anderson out the door and sashayed over to Blake, who was lying on the couch.

Blake was completely enamored with Pet. Her beauty, her intelligence, and her compsure completely staggered him.

"Blake, I know you are recuperating, so I'll go easy on you. First I will make you some lunch. Then I will massage everywhere but around your heart. How does that sound?"

"Sounds good, Pet, but I am very tired."

Pet went into the kitchen and made some soup. Blake was completely sacked out on the couch. Pet covered him and saved some soup for later. She then called Blank and gave him an update. Blake slept until the next morning.

49

Blake woke up the next morning and felt Pet right next to him. "Hey, Pet, how did you get me up here?"

"Blank came over and helped me. How do you feel?"

"He didn't see me naked, did he? I don't have any clothes on."

"No he didn't," she said. "But there's a reason you don't have clothes on. Wanna eat first?"

"Uh, maybe I can wait a few minutes."

"Good. I've waited a bloody long time for a little action."

And action they had.

Blake went downstairs two hours later and downed soup and a bologna sandwich. Pet had to go to work, and so did Blake. He thought about Blank coming to his home and helping Pet. It sounded crazy to him, but Pet was worth it. At least he thought so most of the time.

Also eating at the table was Anderson. Blake knew his whole life had changed.

Blake and Anderson went to his office the next Monday afternoon to meet with Rex. "Hi, Rex. Any news from Chicago?"

"Yes, actually. Snook did a good job. There were some that wanted to retire or leave and eight that want to stay. I recommend seven of them. All seven want to go to New York. Actually, I would recommend we keep two of them in Chicago, as you suggested, in a small office under the direction of New York."

"Let's do that for now. Let's lay off the one guy, keep two writers, the ones closest to the Chicago teams, in Chicago, and ship the rest to New York. Give the employees sixty days to make the move and pay them for their expenses. Buy their existing residences if you have to. And then sell them."

"I'll do it, Blake. I am experiencing a renewed vigor on the digital paper. Give me a week to give you a rough draft of how it might work and the costs."

"If you need more time, take it. We have to get this right."

"You bet, Blake. See you soon."

Blake and Anderson traveled the twenty feet to Blake's new office and asked Liz to come in. "Hi, Liz. How do you like your new office?"

"Good, Blake, but Pet called and wants to see you. On business!"

"Okay. Everything going well?"

"Really good," replied Liz. "Rex is really into it. He should be your right-hand man. He is, and he's good."

"Good to hear. Remember, it's your job to keep me informed. I want to know everything that's going on."

"The last weekly magazine just came out. I put one on your desk," said Liz. "It looks good. The next issue will feature you on the cover as the new owner."

"No, I'll write a half-page story. Put a small picture at the top of page 3 and emphasize Rex as the operator on the same page. I want sports on the cover. Any mail?"

"Yes, forty-five letters asking for money. Two long lost relatives, and channel 11 wants to interview you. Here is the name and number. Before you say no, it would be great publicity. Our advertising department could use it."

"Maybe," said Blake. "I really don't like to be the celebrity. I like to write about them!"

"Yes, but it is the way it is. Someone blabbed it to the public."

Anderson chimed in. "Mr. Brennon. I will be happy to have some investigators find out who squealed, but as you know, there are a million people to choose from. Lottery people, your lawyer, the magazine employees, the—"

"I got it, Tim. Call me Blake, please. It's no use. The cat is out of the bag, and we have to deal with it."

Blake called Pet and said Blank wanted to talk to

him about proceeding with the cheerleader murder case. "Pet, tell Blank I will see him tomorrow morning at ten. In the meantime, come over tonight?"

"Can't tonight, Blake. Maybe tomorrow night. We'll see."

Blake hung up and decided to go to the high school and question the principal and people there again—along with Anderson of course. As luck would have it, he saw Vicki in the hallway to the principal's office. "Well, hello, Vicki. Nice to see you without your hoods with you."

"I see you have your hood with you, Mr. Brennon. I asked you not to continue with this. I was just called in to talk to Assistant Principal. He asked me more questions!"

Blake interrupted. "You know I didn't even suspect the Blades. Now they are at the top of the list."

"We didn't do it. But my dudes don't like you nosing around. You gotta stop before it's too late. I just found out you have enough money. Why jeopardize your health?"

"What does that mean, Vicki?"

"Nothing, just a friendly warning. Go count your money. Or better yet, give me some, and I will count it for you."

"I don't have any left. The magazine took all my money," said Blake.

"Sorry, Charley. I know you got a lot left. Don't bull-shit me."

"Wouldn't dream of it. By the way, how's your boyfriend?"

"If you mean Johnny, we were never really a couple. He keeps hanging around. I'm trying to get rid of him, but he's a bigwig in our club. I gotta go to my next class. Watch your ass, Brennon."

Blank said Johnny was coming into his office. Blake drove to the sheriff's office to be in on the conversation. It was a good thing Blake's and the sheriff's offices were so close.

"Thank you for coming in, Johnny," said Blank.

"Did I have a choice? A policeman said to get in his car."

"I'll have to talk to him, Johnny. While you're here, we just have a few questions for you. Just trying to get ahead of the murder," said Blank. "We think the Blades had something to do with this murder. Any idea why they would want to terminate this girl's life?"

"They didn't kill her. And that reporter standing over there doesn't know what he's talking about," said Johnny.

"We think someone in your gang did it. It has nothing to do with Mr. Brennon. That's what we think."

"Why would we want to do that? This is harassment!"

"We don't think you ever wanted it to happen. If you help us, we will put in a good word to the DA for you. Just tell us why it happened."

"It didn't happen by the Blades. And we are not a gang. We are a club."

"Mr. Brennon said you kidnapped him and threatened him."

Johnny paused and seemed shaken by the questions. "We just talked to him. He came over to our clubhouse."

"Oh, so you were there, along with all of your buddies and Vicki?"

"He came to see Vicki. We just strolled in. Purely a coincidence."

"Just to get this straight, you didn't pull a knife on him?"

"What knife?" asked Johnny.

"The one the officer took from you when you came in."

"That's just for whittling. No. Never did that."

"Oh, by the way," continued Blank, "Vicki says you are not her boyfriend and wishes for you to stop bugging her."

"Oh yeah? Well, I've done a lot for her. She is really ungrateful. But that is none of your business."

"Well, it depends on what you've done for her or participated in doing."

"Come on, Sheriff. The club didn't do anything, and Vicki didn't do anything. They didn't like Rebecca. She was a Goody Two-shoes who shouldn't have made the squad ahead of Vicki. But you think the Blades would kill her? Come on!"

Blake then bluffed. "Johnny, one of your club mates told a different story. Do you want to change your story now? Later will be too late."

"No, Blake. Sorry you felt uncomfortable. The Blades always try to be hospitable."

"Okay, Johnny. We got your statement on tape. The officer will drive you back."

"Will he give me my knife back?" asked Johnny as he glared at Blake.

"After we check it out against other crimes," said Blank. "Check back with us in a couple of months. We are really backlogged."

Johnny left, and Blake talked to Blank. "Blank, he never said *we* about the Blades and referred to them as *they*. Do you think that means anything?"

"I don't know, Blake, but someone in that club did it. Yet the motive to help Vicki is a weak motive."

"I know, Blank, but we are on the right track. Let's keep it up."

"Let's continue to work together. We'll solve it. But you better go now. Your babysitter is sitting in the lobby."

Blake left, waved at Pet, and talked to Anderson on the way to the *Register*'s office.

"I told you about our conversation with Johnny. What do you think?" asked Blake.

"I just don't know if he's capable of violence, enough to really hurt you, Blake. But in a group, he might be able to do anything. Do you have any more intel on the Blades?"

"I've given you everything, including the sheriff's intel. They just aren't that big or noticeable. The ones still in high school go to class usually, most of them, and get decent grades. A few minor scrapes with the law. Except one, the older guy they call Rats. He seems to run the gang. The others seem to look up to him, including Johnny. The only girl I've seen in the club is Vicki. I just don't know."

"Well, you better be cautious. You said he glared at you. I don't like that."

"Drop me off at the office and then go home. I'll be there for a few hours."

"No can do," said Anderson. "But I will go home until this afternoon, and I will send my replacement over now. I don't want to sound paranoid or give you a reason to keep my employ, but I've guarded several people with a much smaller problem than you have on at least two fronts, including your newly acquired wealth."

"I understand, Tim. That would be great."

Tim Anderson waited for his replacement, and Blake went into his office. He hadn't spent much time in it since it was remodeled. Blake asked Liz and Rex to come in.

"Okay, people. Where are we?"

Rex told him the transition to the bimonthly paper issue had started. He gave Blake a list of suggested subscription options, including the digital option that would be in full bloom by the end of the month. All customers with the paper subscription also got the digital version included.

Option letters to the Chicago employees had been

sent, and a reply date of two weeks had been asked for. The Chicago lease had two years left, and the landlord gave the *Register* a reasonable buyout to leave early. The same landlord had a much smaller executive office available with two offices and a reception quarters, with a bathroom down the hall. Blake told Rex to have the two writers who would work there check it out, and if they liked it, he should close the deal.

Blake talked about a dozen more items and dismissed Rex. Liz stayed.

"Anything new, Liz?"

"Yes. I have six items concerning your financial situations. One is from Dwight Spenser, your attorney, about a gift to the Rotary Club. I thought you might want to talk to him about that in person. The others are outlined in memos. Employee and other problems go to Rex, and you if necessary, and outstanding achievements will go to him and then to you. You, of course, will get progress reports almost daily. Other items are noted on your memos, and I will talk to you about other stuff in a minute."

"I thought this was going to entail a lot for you. Remember, if you need an assistant or secretary ... In fact, get us a secretary that can do a lot of the secretarial work. You will be my assistant."

"Okay, Blake. I have someone who is working here in mind. Susie."

"Yes, she'd be great. But run it past Rex first and tell him to replace her if she agrees to work with us."

Blake and Liz talked for two more hours. Liz said Susie had already agreed. Time to go see Dwight Spenser.

Blake and Anderson's replacement, Ed, drove to Spenser's office and were told to go right in.

"Hi, Dwight," said Blake. The two chatted for a few minutes. Blake told Ed to go wait outside and then got down to Rotary business.

"You mentioned donating to the Rotary Club. Any money left?" asked Spenser.

"A little. Do you think a one-million donation would be cool?"

"Can I suggest two hundred and fifty thousand? See how it goes and add to it later? The 501c nonprofit organization is all set up. I just want to see how we Rotarians handle it."

"I'll write you a check."

"No, how about giving it to the club at tomorrow's meeting. Everyone wants to know where you are these days."

"Just lazy, I guess. Tomorrow would be perfect."

By the next day Ed had switched with Anderson, then Ed again, and then Anderson, who accompanied Blake to the Rotary meeting at the Naval Golf Course catering building. Blake shook everyone's hands. About thirty members were there. President Jesse then introduced Blake as the speaker for the afternoon.

"Hi, you all. As most of you know, I've been a member for fifteen years. The international organization and this group has been great. Fundraising has been challenging, but we've also raised money from the community. A lot of the funds have come out of our pockets. My hope is that some of that burden will be lifted from you. I am donating two hundred and fifty thousand dollars tax-free to this club. If you come up with a more expensive project, Dwight will bring it to me for consideration.

"As you know, I have come into some money and will, for the time being, channel most donations through this club. We will undoubtedly get a lot more members, but it is this group that I will fondly remember the most. I will make as many meetings as I can, but things are pretty hectic right now.

"I have purchased the *Sports Register Magazine.* As many of you know, I worked for them for fifteen years. The magazine will make some changes that I think will make it even better. One change is that Rotary International and our club, will have a half-page ad every issue. Free of charge. I wish us good luck and hope to continue helping our community and this country. Through Rotary International, we help the world too, as you know."

Blake got a standing ovation from the twenty men and ten women. He got a special Paul Harris award from Rotary International, via President Jesse, for outstanding service to Rotary. Paul Harris started Rotary in Chicago in 1905. Blake thought Harris might not have understood closing the Chicago office like he did.

Blake sat down and finished his lunch. He was proud of the Rotary Club and the fact that he was able to help them help others. But after that, it was back home. He and Anderson made the trek from Garden Grove to Newport Beach. It was a good day. It would be a good night too. Pet was coming over.

50

A couple of weeks passed, and Blake wondered if he had to have a bodyguard anymore.

"It's up to you," said Anderson. "I think it's a small price to pay to be safe. People are money hungry and even envy you that you won. And then there are the Blades."

"Yes, I know. I haven't heard from them for two weeks. Let's keep it for about a week more. After then maybe cut it down some."

Blade and the sheriff made no progress on the cheerleader murder. It looked like the Blades, but they needed proof. The Blades could be prosecuted for threatening Blake, but Blake and the sheriff could wait and hope to get them for murder.

The next morning, Blake and Anderson left Blake's house as usual and ate breakfast at Tommy Pastramis—a great pastrami place that had good breakfast as well.

There were only four people there. Anderson and Blake sat down at one of the tables.

Just then, four men came in. One stabbed Anderson in the gut, making him helpless. The other three grabbed Blake and dragged him to a van. Then Blake was knocked unconscious and thrown into the van. The van took off.

The customers and employees at Tommy's sat frozen, as everything happened in a very short period. Anderson was bleeding profusely.

Blake woke up in a shabby room. His head was throbbing. It took about twenty minutes to get his wits about him. He was in his underwear. What was going on?

Just then, a familiar face came into the room. It was Rats, the head guy from the Blades.

"Hello, Mr. Brennon. Have a headache? That's for accusing us of killing someone. But you're here for a different reason. You'll know about that tomorrow."

"Well, Rats. Where are we? Looks like your club-house. Why am I naked?" asked Blake.

"We found out you are a master at electronics," replied Rats. "We had to make sure you weren't hiding anything. You aren't. Here, you can put your pants back on. Here's your shirt too. I'll keep your shoes in case you try to run. But we have a lot of people just outside and around the place."

Rats left, leaving Blake alone. Blake could tell there were people outside. The walls and door were thin, at least the inside walls and door. Blake's cobwebs were going away now. He thought he might be in a basement. There were no windows and no other doors. *That rock don't roll,* he thought.

After another couple of hours, another familiar face came in. It was Vicki. She brought in a hamburger and french fries and a soda. She looked around like she was very nervous. What happened to the confident girl he knew?

"Mr. Brennon, I'm so sorry. I don't like you, but this is going too far. Here is your dinner."

"Vicki, get me out of here. I'll give you a hundred thousand dollars!"

"I wish I could, Mr. Brennon. But no one trusts anyone around here. They are watching me. I overheard Rats say I was the weakest link."

"Call my magazine. Talk to Liz or Rex."

Vicki was crying now. "I can't, Blake. They would kill me."

"Go home. Tell your parents. Please, Vicki."

Vicki replied, "I haven't been home in two days. This whole thing got out of hand. Other guys are running the show. I'm no saint, but this isn't—"

Just then, Johnny came in. "Come on, Vicki. Give him the burger and get out of here. What are you crying about? You know it has to be this way."

Johnny pulled Vicki out of the room. He could hear

them going up some stairs to other rooms. There was one lamp with no shade and a lightbulb. That was it. Not a mattress or chair, only an old couch. Blake thought this was a real pickle. Blake fell asleep on the couch. It was a very uneasy sleep, and he woke up the next morning. He didn't know what time it was. What was going to happen today?

Later, two men came in. Both were dressed immaculately in suits and ties. They entered the room and stood by Blake, who was sitting on the couch.

"Good morning, Mr. Brennon. Do you want to get out alive?"

"That would be nice. Who are you?"

"You can call me Mutt, and that's Jeff. We want one million dollars. Unmarked, not traceable. You get the idea?"

"How am I going to get that kind of money cooped up in here?"

"I have a feeling you can get it. Oh, by the way, get another fifty thousand for these kids here. They have been very helpful," said Mutt.

"Get me a phone," said Blake.

"Oh, we don't want to put you out. Write a letter. We'll suggest some things. Tell us who we should see," said Jeff.

Blake wrote a letter to Rex. Mutt and Jeff didn't leave the room. Blake gave them the letter. Mutt and Jeff approved.

"Mr. Brennon. If all of this goes well, you might live through this."

"Is Tim Anderson okay?"

"Your sitter? Don't know. The kids got a little anxious. They said he was dead."

"I can't control this being cooped up here," stated Blake.

"We can't control you if you aren't. Sorry, Charlie," said Jeff.

The two left the room with the letter in hand, making sure to lock the door behind them.

A little later, Vicki came into the room with another hamburger.

"How about a bathroom?" asked Blake.

"I've been told to tell you to go in your pants," said Vicki.

"So, the two big boys are calling the shots, huh, Vicki?"

"They approached Rats and Johnny. Said they would pay us fifty thousand dollars to get you here and guard you for a few days."

"Do you get any more for killing my bodyguard?"

"It was his fault. He tried to protect you and pulled his gun. Rats said he had to stab him."

"Is this what you signed up for?" asked Blake.

"No, it isn't, Mr. Brennon. The boys have roughed up a few people and stole some. But I didn't know they were like this!"

"Did you know those guys are asking for one million dollars and another fifty thousand for the Blades?"

"I think most of us just want to get out of this, Mr. Brennon. All except Johnny and Rats."

"Then let's all leave. Mutt and Jeff have just left your house, right?" asked Blake.

"They said they will kill us if we don't keep our part of the bargain. And they mean it. They said we would all be dead in two days if they were betrayed."

Blake pondered what to say next. "Listen, Vicki. You said the Blades never killed before. What about Rebecca?"

"I don't think you are going to live, Mr. Brennon. I heard them say you know way too much and have too many resources to let it go. So I can tell you, Johnny strangled Rebecca."

"Did you ask him to?" asked Blake.

"No. Not at all. I am really mad at him. He knew how much I wanted to be a cheerleader. It was to be something positive in my life. I told him I would do anything to make the squad. But I never meant anything like this. Please believe me, Mr. Brennon."

"Whenever I saw you both the last few weeks, you were always arguing. What gives?" asked Blake.

Vicki started to cry again. "I guess he thought he deserved to be my boyfriend. He got me into the Blades, he got rid of my cheer competition, he proved himself to me. But when I found out, I told him to stay away. He didn't. He even said he could do the same thing to me as he did to Rebecca."

"I can see why your parents didn't think you could have been in on this," said Blake.

"I don't know about now. I haven't been home. I'm sure they called the police."

"Do they know about this place?" asked Blake.

"Oh no. They would be furious if they knew. By the way, Mr. Brennon, I overheard everyone saying the two guys offered an additional fifty thousand to waste you. No one answered. I guess they are thinking about it."

Blake paused again and said, "Vicki, you have to help me get out of this place. If I'm killed, you are part of it."

Vicki started crying again. "I can't. They are always watching me."

Johnny came busting though the door and asked if Vicki was playing Monopoly with Blake. He grabbed Vicki and pushed her out the door again.

Blake peed his pants for more than one reason.

Blake thought about what Vicki had said. It seemed feasible. Did she put him up to it? Blake's gut told him no. Just then, Johnny came into the room.

"Mr. Brennon, what has Vicki been telling you?"

"Nothing much. How about letting me go for fifty thousand dollars?"

"No, Mr. Brennon. You would have me behind bars in ten minutes."

"I just want to go home. One hundred thousand dollars, and that's my final offer," said Blake.

"Mutt said you have enough on me to know I killed Rebecca. But you have to know that I wanted Vicki real bad. I love her. I got her into this club. I got her on the cheer squad that she always wanted. And when she found out how I did all that, including getting rid of Rebecca, she cut me off. Doesn't even want to look at me."

"A jury will go easy on you. Temporary insanity. Lovestruck," lied Blake.

"Don't bullshit me, Mr. Brennon. Besides, you won't be around to snitch on me. When Mutt and Jeff get the million, they really don't want anybody around that knows them."

"But they are at my office now," said Blake. "Everyone will know them when they ask for a million bucks."

"They have some great disguises on, Mr. Brennon. And don't count on your office helping you out. Mutt and Jeff said they will have you killed if they are stopped."

"What about you, Johnny? What about everyone else in your gang? Do you really think they will trust you to forget about them?"

"Hey, they said we could have a continuing relationship," said Johnny. "They said you might try and come between us. And I will need them to skip town. I'm taking Vicki with me, like it or not!"

"Johnny, don't be a fool. These guys are pros. They will eat you for lunch."

"It's been a ball chatting with you, Mr. Brennon. They should be back soon with your million. Too bad you had to stick your nose in this."

An hour passed, and no Mutt and Jeff. Then there was a loud sound. It was the front door crashing in and a lot of shouting. Within seconds, the door to his prison was opened, and a welcome sight came through it. It was Sheriff Blank. Many deputies behind him were rounding up everyone in the house.

"Cut it a little close, didn't you, Blank?"

"I had to make sure Rex handed the two bad guys the money and they accepted it to make sure we could make the extortion stick."

"How about kidnapping? And did Anderson die?"

"No. He's getting better. It was touch and go for a while. He wants to see you. He's actually awake today."

"I'm so happy. By the way, go easy on Vicki. Put her in a secure room at the jail. I want to sort out her involvement."

"I gotta hear this," said Blank. "I thought she might be the murderer."

"No. Johnny did it. He confessed when he thought I wouldn't make it past today. I don't think he would have made it either. By the way, where are Mutt and Jeff?"

"They took a little trip downtown and are in isolation.

They sure look funny in all that makeup. They were sure surprised when we came in."

"I'll go with you now and make my rather lengthy statement."

Blake saw Vicki sobbing in the corner. She looked at Blake as if to say she was sorry. Blake still didn't know if he could believe her. He also passed Johnny, who asked, "What happened? How did the police know you were even here?" Blake told him it was age and experience. He wasn't going to tell him the truth about his GPS.

Blake asked Blank to make a very big detour so he could shower, change clothes, and shave. Blank obliged. The hospital Anderson was in was on the way to the sheriff's office, and again Blank relented and stopped for a few minutes. Blake would talk to Anderson again soon. Anderson looked beat up, but he was able to say a few words to Blake.

Then it was back at the station, Pet went running up to Blake, gave him a big kiss, and ordered him into her office.

"I won't need to see you, Blake, for about a half hour," said Blank.

"Good. Because I do! Get in here, Blake!" said Pet.

"Hi, Pet. I've had a rough couple of days."

"It's going to be rougher if you don't tell me what happened."

"You know most of it, Pet."

"There are some holes. Start at the beginning," ordered Pet.

"Well, you know I hired Tim Anderson to be my bodyguard. Well, he and Rex and I devised a plan in case I was kidnapped by the Blades or anyone else. Really, the thought of extortion was really secondary.

"Remember the heart operation I had not too long ago? Well, it entailed my main artery. I had a GPS installed with the help of a stent. Rex, Blank, and Anderson would always know where I was. So, we thought that I might be kidnapped again, but I didn't think those kids could pull it off. They couldn't have if it hadn't been orchestrated by those two hoods. Very professional hoods—just not very well versed in the latest technology. They stripped me when I came in and took away my pens and everything I had on me. They were satisfied I was clean. Luckily, they didn't check my artery. Then Blank and the deputies rescued me."

"You forgot to mention Anderson was almost killed, and you were knocked out," said Pet.

"Yes, they were on us in a hurry. And those stupid kids didn't care who was watching. Mutt and Jeff stayed at the gang house and waited for us. I have to go now and talk to Blank."

Blake walked into Blank's office. Blank had a tape recorder. Blake told him the whole story and then talked specifics about the cheerleader murder case.

"I talked to Vicki," said Blank. "I know we talked in the car on the way over here about her involvement. What's your final feeling about it?"

"I don't think she told Johnny to kill Rebecca. She might have asked him to scare her off the team and might even have pretended to like him for that, and she was happy when he got her into the Blades. She regrets all of that, as Johnny was really pissed that she spurned him."

"I will have Johnny interviewed to hear his story. I'll let you know what I think after that. What do you think we should do with Vicki?" asked Blank.

"I think she should plead guilty to some minor things, quit the cheer squad, and be put on probation for two years. Any problems at all, and she goes down. Her parents have a lawyer. Please see if the DA will buy it. Then let me know. In the meantime, how about OR for her and let her parents take her home? Even though a lot of it is her fault, let's give her a break if she cooperates."

"What about the kidnapping of you *twice* by the Blades?" asked Blank.

"Throw the book at them, except for Vicki. The Blades put a knife into a nice guy just doing his job. Tell the DA I will see him if he wants me to. By the way, Rats and Johnny are the real bad guys. And of course Mutt and Jeff."

"Okay, Blake," said Blank. "I agree. Come in the day after tomorrow, and we'll go over it again. That will give me time to interrogate everyone and be better informed. Meanwhile, someone wants to drive you home."

Pet was waiting for Blake. She took him to Blake's condo.

51

Blake admired Pet from across the room. She had an hourglass figure and always seemed to be as sexy and flirtatious as she could be. Like now, as she came over to nurse Blake back to health.

"Pet, I'm really okay. It was an ordeal, but I'm good."

"Good to hear, Blake." She took her clothes off in the sensuous Pet way and helped Blake out of his. Whatever reservations he had about Pet were gone. Pet was there now just for him. And she proved it. That rock was really starting to roll.

Pet nursed Blake back for two days. It was time to see Blank and Anderson. Pet drove Blake and Anderson to the sheriff's office.

Blank started the conversation. "You're looking good, Blake. Did Pet take good care of you? I'm sure she did. Mr. and Mrs. Nguyen and Vicki came in yesterday. They all agreed to testify against the Blades and Mutt and Jeff, and Johnny. Their lawyer was here with them, and they all agreed to probation. The school has already kicked her off the cheer squad and put her in their continuation school. She will be there for the rest of her junior and senior years if she complies entirely with the plea bargain. We would drop the kidnapping charges. She will be on probation for three years. The DA said he would go along with all this."

"Good," said Blake. "Do you concur that we can give her a break?"

"If you can, I can. Her parents were furious at her. Her lawyer and Vicki were conciliatory. She will help our case against Mutt and Jeff. The Blades will be no more. Rats and Johnny will be prosecuted to the fullest. We'll see about the other Blades after going over your report. By the way, Rats is the one who clobbered you."

"What did Johnny and Rats say?"

"Rats said to fuck myself, so guess what I'm going to do to him? Johnny needs psychiatric help. We'll go that route. His public defender agrees. Rebecca's family will go along with everything too. They told me to tell you thank you for everything you did. By the way, I thank you too. Ever thought about being a deputy sheriff?"

"No thanks, Blank. I have a sports magazine to run. But let me know if something sports related comes up, and maybe I can be of help. But not for a while."

"I'll be in touch," said Blank. "If anyone doesn't plead

out, I'll need you at their trial. But this is really open and shut."

"Sounds good, Blank. Now I have to go to my office. Pet has offered to take me there and then back home."

"Sounds good, Blake. But don't steal her from me. She's a good officer."

"We'll see," said Blake. "It's up to her."

Blake really wanted to make fewer company decisions and do more writing, his real love. Another trip to SRM.

"So, Rex. You make decisions. If you think I should be involved, let Liz know, and she will let me know right away. You can call me anytime if necessary. But I want to figure out when I will have time to have some fun and write meaningful articles.

"By the way, you did great work getting me out of their gang house, and you probably saved my life. If it happens again, you know what to do. And of course, let's keep the GPS thing our secret."

"You got it, Blake. I see you have a ride home."

"Yes. Thank you for everything."

Blake and Pet went to the hospital.

"Tim. I'm so happy to see you are doing okay."

"I'll be back bugging you soon. I have some different options for your security. We won't be around you twenty-four seven, but you will have fast access to us. I have a nice *special* watch for you. It even tells time!"

Blake knew it had a lot of gadgets on it.

"Good. I understand you helped get me out of serious trouble too. Thank you for that."

"Sure, Blake. I'll stop by as soon as I can get out of this place."

"Great, Tim. By the way, here is a little check and a thank-you card." Anderson said it wasn't necessary but was grateful to Blake.

As Blake and Pet were walking out, she said they had to hurry to Blake's house. She had to tell him something. She looked serious. Blake thought this was the end of their relationship. Was he right all along that he was only good when useful to the sheriff's office?

Pet asked Blake to sit down. Blake was worried.

"I have something to tell you, Blake."

"What?" asked Blake.

Pet answered, "I am pregnant."

CPSIA information can be obtained
at www.ICGtesting.com
Printed in the USA
LVHW010149100221
678885LV00002B/143